THE COWBOY'S HOPE

DIXON RANCH SERIES - BOOK 3

CHRISTINA BUTRUM

Copyright © 2021 by Christina Butrum

All rights reserved.

No part of this book may be reproduced in any form or by any electronic or mechanical means, including information storage and retrieval systems, without written permission from the author, except for the use of brief quotations in a book review.

Edited by: Three Owls Editing

Cover by: Daniel at thebookbrander.com

Formatted by: Christina Butrum

"Love recognizes no barriers. It jumps hurdles, leaps fences, penetrates walls to arrive at its destination full of hope."

―――――

Maya Angelou

CHAPTER ONE

Ashley Carlson tapped her thumbs against the steering wheel as she focused on the long road in front of her. She was running late, pressed for time, and toeing the line between obeying the law and breaking the speed limit. And the good Lord knew getting pulled over and receiving a ticket was the last thing she needed right now.

Her grandfather expected her at the ranch over twenty minutes ago, and she wouldn't have a good reason for being late. Except the morning hadn't gone as planned. According to her plan, she had enough time to see Brycen off to school after eating breakfast together, not to mention being ready for the day herself. But she'd overslept her alarm and fought with Brycen to get ready for his first day at school as she tried to convince him he would make plenty of friends to make up for losing the ones he'd left behind before moving to Woodford Creek.

Letting out a deep sigh, Ashley gripped the steering wheel and tried her best to remain hopeful and focus only on the positive. Moving to Montana was supposed to be a fresh start, a breath of fresh air after what felt like a crashing halt to the life she'd once dreamed of.

Ashley never thought her dreams would become a nightmare so soon after marrying Colin and having her son, Brycen.

Ashley squinted against the mid-morning sun as she headed east on County Road 285. It wouldn't be long before she pulled into the driveway that would lead her to the Dixon Ranch. According to her grandfather's directions, it was just up ahead, over the next hill, and to the left.

She glanced at the clock on the dashboard, counting the minutes that passed. Her grandfather wouldn't be happy with her late arrival. With her mind preoccupied with ways to make things right once she arrived at the ranch, she guided her car over the hill but slammed on the brakes as she jerked the steering wheel to the right to miss the large red cow standing in the middle of the road.

Shrieking, she held on tightly to the steering wheel as her car plummeted into the ditch, rocked and jolted along the uneven ground, and came to a sloshing halt before going head on with a telephone pole.

Ashley's heart raced as she gripped the steering wheel. She looked back over her shoulder in search of the cow she missed colliding with and cursed under her breath as she inhaled a deep breath and released it to calm her frazzled nerves.

Ashley attempted to open the door in order to climb out of the car, but she soon realized, not only was her car now stuck in the ditch but she was stuck in the car as well. She scrambled to find her phone, knowing she had no choice but to call her grandfather and ask for him to come and rescue her.

"Well, good morning, Ashley," her grandfather greeted after the third ring. "I've been expecting—"

"I know, Gramps, and I'm sorry." She released a heavy sigh and said, "I've had a rough start to my morning, and long story short, it just got worse. I need your help."

After a silent pause, she said, "I'm fine, the cow's fine, but my car—"

"Now, wait a minute, Ash," her grandfather said, "did you say cow?"

Ashley tipped her head back, resting it against the seat. She knew her grandfather would have a hard time believing it. Ashley couldn't blame him. She hadn't expected a cow to be the one to derail her morning, either. Speaking of which, she couldn't wait to have a word or two with the owner of the cow.

"Yes, Gramps, a cow," Ashley said and explained the gist of what happened. "Can you send someone to help me out of the ditch?"

She looked over her shoulder, searching for the cow who was now meandering her way along the side of the road, grazing and paying no mind to the trouble she caused.

"I'll send one of the Dixon boys your way," her grandfather stated matter-of-factly. Ashley tried her best to talk him into coming to her rescue instead, a failed attempt at saving herself from embarrassment, but was reminded that he had a job to do. "You'll be in good hands. I'll see you when you get here."

No sooner had Ashley ended the call with her grandfather than she saw a tractor heading her way. She squinted against the morning sun, trying to get a good look at who was behind the wheel. If it was one of the Dixon boys her grandfather promised to send, she had been closer to the Dixon Ranch than she'd realized.

The tractor pulled to the side of the road, and she waited with anticipation. She wanted to get to the ranch and assist her grandfather the best she could with what little she could offer.

Ashley watched as a man wearing a cowboy hat climbed out of the tractor and approached her car. He tipped his hat in greeting with a slight smirk on his face as she rolled the window down and offered a friendly hello.

"Doc Thompson says you're in need of some help," he said. "I'd say he's right."

Aside from his smirk and the chuckle he let out after observing the mess she was in, she was relieved to know he was there to help her out of the situation she'd gotten herself into. She would be sure to thank him as soon as she was on solid ground.

"If it hadn't been for the cow standing in the middle of the road, I wouldn't be sitting where I am right now," she said, trying her best to keep her frustrations under control as she pointed out the culprit leading to her mishap.

The man looked over at the cow that was nonchalantly walking away from the scene it caused. He let out a laugh as he pointed in its direction. "Big Red?"

"Big Red? The cow has a name?" She raised a brow, making the connection that he somehow knew the cow. Good. He would know the owner. "Big Red shouldn't have been standing in the middle of the road. If it hadn't been for that cow, I would be assisting my grandfather by now. The owner should learn how to keep his livestock where it belongs."

"Well, I suppose I should introduce myself," he said, offering her a wink. "I'm Blake Dixon and happen to be the owner of that cow and Dixon Ranch."

Ashley sunk back in her seat as she looked up at the man who she now knew to be the owner she thought about giving a piece of her mind to. Except now, she thought twice about that as he stood by and waited to assist with getting her car out of the ditch.

There had been a sense of urgency to get her car back on the road, but now that she had stuck her foot in her mouth, she wanted to crawl away and hide from the man who had come to her rescue.

"Put the car in neutral and be ready to brake. I'll get to work on getting this thing back on the road."

"Thank you," she said. She watched in the rearview mirror and waited for him to hook the chains.

He stood up and clapped the dirt from his hands before telling her, "Just sit tight, and remember what I said about being ready to brake."

She nodded with a relieved smile, feeling bad for being frustrated with the man and his cow. She would choose her battles. This was one of those instances where she needed to just thank God she didn't get hurt and let go of the anger she'd felt before Blake had arrived.

It would be only a matter of time before he had her car out of the ditch and back on the road.

Waiting for a signal, she found herself preoccupied with the man's appearance. If she had to guess, he was in his mid-thirties, much like her, and was used to getting his hands dirty. The sleeves of his flannel shirt pulled taut against his arms and exposed working muscles as he yanked on the chain. With muscles like that, there was no doubt in her mind he earned his keep at the ranch.

A loud thump pulled her attention away from the toned muscles as she focused on his face. How long had he been just standing there waiting for her to notice?

She rolled her window down and tried to hide her embarrassment.

"I'm ready to get you out of there," he stated matter-of-factly. "Just remember what I said. Be ready to brake once I get you out."

Ashley gave a quick nod and waited for him to climb onto the tractor before shifting the car into neutral. She tried her best to relax her nerves as she waited for the tractor to fire up. She didn't know a thing about tractors, and she had never gone into a ditch. Even though it was quite embarrassing, she shrugged it off, knowing there was a first time for everything, and she wouldn't be in the spot she was in if it hadn't been for that silly cow, anyway.

A sudden jerk caught her off guard and slammed her into the steering wheel. In the side mirror, Blake kept a steady hand on the tractor's steering wheel as he gave it gas. He glanced over his shoulder every so often to check on her. She could only hope the chain wouldn't break and she would be out of there any minute.

Another sudden jerk on the chain nudged her against the steering wheel, and she wondered if maybe she should have put on the seatbelt. She tried her best to stay focused on Blake, watching for any sign of what to expect, but before she knew it, her car was out of the ditch and colliding with the back of Blake's tractor.

She should have known better than to lose focus. Blake had given her one job, and she blew it.

She pressed on the brake and shifted the car into park before climbing out of the driver's seat. Blake hopped off the tractor and planted his cowboy boots on the ground in front of her. "Did you forget where the brake was?"

She tried to hide her embarrassment. "I'm sorry. I—"

"It's fine," Blake said, cutting her off mid sentence. If he was trying to hide his frustration with her, he wasn't good at it. Ashley caught sight of the tension setting in his jaw as he removed his hat and ran a hand through his sweat-matted, dark brown hair.

"Is your tractor okay?" she asked, approaching the tractor and getting a better look. Blake's laugh stopped her mid stride. Only when she tossed him a raised brow, he said, "I wouldn't be too worried about this old thing. I'd be more worried about your car."

Ashley looked from the tractor to the back of her car.

"If you'd like, I can have my brother take a look at it. He's good at fixing things," Blake said, seeming a bit more relaxed. Maybe he felt bad for her.

"If you think he wouldn't mind?"

"Not at all. I'll meet you there," Blake said, pointing toward the Dixon Ranch.

Ashley thanked him again before climbing into the driver's seat. It didn't go unnoticed that Blake had opened the door for her and insisted on shutting it as well.

He had shown a softer side she hadn't expected to see after colliding with him, but she couldn't help but wonder if it had been out of fear of seeing her cry.

Ashley buckled her seatbelt, offered Blake a soft smile, and shifted the car into drive before heading toward the Dixon Ranch, passing an oblivious Big Red on her way.

"As far as I can see, there doesn't appear to be any damage to your car," a younger man wearing a cowboy hat told her after arriving at the ranch.

"Thanks for looking at it, Garrett," her grandfather said, offering the man a slap on the back.

"It could have been a lot worse, Doc," the man Ashley now knew to be Garrett said. "I'm going to round up the cattle and get Big Red back where she belongs. I'm hoping that I'll be able to fix the fence yet again."

"A fence can only be fixed so many times," her grandfather said, offering Garrett a quick slap on the shoulder before turning his attention back to her. "I'm just glad that you're alright and Blake could get you here safe and sound."

Ashley glanced over her shoulder at the sound of footsteps on gravel behind her. Blake walked up and stood to the side of her and her grandfather. She wasn't sure she owed thanks to Blake for having a cow on the loose, but she owed him for pulling her out of a mess.

"Did my brother look at your car?" Blake asked, searching for any sign of Garrett. "From what I could tell, other than a grill full of ditch weed and mud, there wasn't any damage."

"He looked at it while you were putting the tractor away," her grandfather said. "No damage to be reported. I'm just glad she's okay."

The men talked amongst themselves as though Ashley wasn't standing there. She let them carry on, talking about how she ended up in the ditch in the first place and carrying on about Big Red wreaking havoc.

"Well, I think it's safe to say my morning is off to a rough start," she intervened, letting go of some of the bitterness she felt creeping in. She hated to think of what could have happened if she had been going faster than she was. She had done the best she could to avoid hitting the cow, even though that meant taking the ditch. She'd learned years ago not to swerve, but her instinct kicked in and she didn't have much of a choice in the matter. "I can only hope Brycen isn't having the same luck as I am."

Blake turned to walk away but stopped short when she mentioned her son. "Brycen?"

"Her son," her grandfather said, filling in the pieces and leaving no room for Ashley to talk for herself. Her grandfather was set in his old ways, but she still loved him with her whole heart.

Smiling, silently telling her grandfather she would take it from there, she said, "Brycen is my ten-year-old son. I sent him off this morning for his first day at a new school."

"Ah, I see," Blake said, kicking gravel with the toe of his boot.

She wasn't sure if she bored him with conversation or if he wasn't sure what to add to it, so she gave him an out. "I'm sure you have plenty of work to do around here, so I should leave you to it.

Thanks again for helping me out. I owe you big time."

Blake's gaze met hers, and with a smile, he said, "Don't worry about it. It was no trouble at all."

She turned to head in the direction she'd seen her grandfather walk off to, but stopped when Blake called out, "I'll make sure my brother fixes the fence line to keep Big Red where she belongs."

"That's a good idea."

She smiled as she walked off toward the barn she'd seen her grandfather walk into. He had yet to ask her the details about her morning leading up to the accident, and she couldn't wait to tell him all about it. But first, she needed to learn what they expected of her at the Dixon Ranch.

CHAPTER TWO

Blake Dixon shook his head and let out a low grunt as he watched the woman walk off toward the barn. He couldn't help but wonder what her story was and why she was at his ranch. Of course, she was Doc's granddaughter, so he supposed it made sense that she was there just for a visit. But didn't she say today was her son's first day at a new school?

It didn't matter, anyway. Blake had other things to worry about with Jack Frost right around the corner, and not to mention predators searching the perimeters for young calves and mothers to prey on.

Garrett nudged him in the arm with his elbow, pulling him from his thoughts. "I can't believe Big Red caused such a ruckus," Garrett said. "We've got to do something about that fence. I'm not sure there's anything readily available to keep that cow where she belongs."

"She's just used to roaming free," Blake said. "She's got a mind of her own and nothing will stop her when she's set out to do something. She's a feisty one when she doesn't get her way."

Garrett grabbed a pair of gloves from his back pocket as Blake stayed focused on the barn Ashley had walked into. "One of these days she's going to cause some major damage, and we're going to pay for it," Garrett stated matter-of-factly as he tugged the pair of work gloves onto his hands. "I'm just thankful Ashley wasn't hurt during the fiasco. Doc wouldn't have been too happy knowing his granddaughter wouldn't be able to work alongside him and assist him here at the ranch."

Blake pulled his attention from the barn and focused on Garrett for a minute. He'd heard his brother loud and clear, even though he figured Garrett hadn't meant for that part to slip. "What do you mean to assist him?" Blake asked, keeping his voice low but his tone sharp. He was more than just the owner of the place. Blake was the boss and the bookkeeper. He kept things in line when things tried to get out of hand. He also knew after the hard hit with taxes last spring, the ranch was still trying to recuperate and regain traction. It hadn't helped that their Uncle Curt had hired an accountant who didn't know up from down. It was only when Blake took over that he realized the woman had messed everything up and they had been running in the red for quite some time. "Whose idea was that? And when was it going to be run past me?"

Garrett offered nothing more than a slight shrug before dodging a bullet. "That, I don't know," he said as he grabbed a toolbox and placed it on the four wheeler. "But what I know is, Doc won't be around forever and it's good to see the old man has some help."

Blake thought about it for a minute as Garrett prepared the things he needed to mend another broken fence. If Ashley was there to assist her grandfather in providing vet care to his livestock, Blake would have thought he would have been the first to know. He knew Doc was getting older, but he was still sharp. Wise enough to know that he should have mentioned bringing one more person onto the ranch. Blake didn't like the thought of giving up a spare cabin he might need later down the road for a ranch hand.

"Didn't think it was that big of a deal," Garrett said with a shrug as he climbed on top of the four wheeler. He didn't give Blake a chance to say a word before heading off toward the pasture with the broken fence line.

Blake understood where his brother could get off thinking it wasn't a big deal, but money was tight on the ranch. Something his brothers knew little about because Blake kept the ranch's finances to himself. This year's winter was going to be one of the worst ones yet, and they still needed to figure out a way to keep their cattle safe from the wolf packs circling the ranch late at night. Not to mention paying extra to the ranch hands for providing hourly checks on the birthing cows a few months from now.

He couldn't afford to pay for someone extra to do the same job as Doc Thompson. No matter who she was or what her story was.

With a subtle grunt, Blake grabbed his hat and ran a hand through his matted hair. He checked his watch for the time. Mama Dixon and Becca would have lunch ready within the next hour. He assumed he had plenty of time to talk to Doc when the man wasn't elbow-deep with the birthing process.

He walked up the snow-covered hill toward the barn he'd watched Ashley disappear to. If she was assisting Doc like Garrett had mentioned, Blake would ask her to step out so he can have a word with Doc. The only problem was Blake didn't know how to approach the subject without knowing Ashley's story and why she was there. She seemed too much like a city girl to be there at the ranch. Not that city girls didn't make good ranchers. Becca and Shyann had proved him wrong time and time again.

He tugged at his flannel jacket, flipping the collar

up and pulling it closer to the back of his neck. Temperatures were dropping to the mid-to-low forties as they approached November. One more subtle reminder that he wasn't prepared for the harsh winter months ahead.

Blake rapped his knuckles on the barn door before giving it a shove. Both Doc and Ashley were standing near the newest mama in the herd. The calf had been born in the middle of the night, and thankfully Mason had been following through with his hourly checks. If he hadn't been an honest worker, the calf wouldn't have made it.

"How's she doing?" Blake asked, taking a few steps toward the gate.

"She's doing much better," Doc said, giving Blake an assuring grin. "Ashley here has helped calm the mama down with some of those whatchamacallits—"

"Oils, Gramps," Ashley said, smiling with a subtle shake of her head as she looked at Blake. "I've brought a few things along with me, at least what I could fit in my car, and my calming herbs and oils were among the first to be packed."

Blake looked to Doc for some kind of clue why the woman would use herbs and oils on his livestock, but the old man offered a sly smile and went about checking over the young calf and its mama.

"Do you mind if I have a word with Doc?" Blake asked, trying his best to be polite and not show his annoyance. He was old school. And he knew for a fact that Doc was old school as well. He wasn't sure what herbs and oils Ashley had up her sleeve, but Blake wasn't interested in finding out. That stuff didn't work as pharmaceuticals did. Cattle weren't close to domesticated cats and dogs. So whatever Ashley was used to treating in the city, she had another think coming there on the ranch. If she was there that long. "Mama Dixon and Becca will have lunch ready if you'd like to head to the main house."

Ashley looked at Doc for the okay to head inside, and the man went along with Blake's order. "I'll meet you there, Ash. Give us a few minutes."

With that, Ashley nodded and said, "I should probably call the moving company and find out where the moving truck is at."

Blake stood off to the side, shocked at the mention of a moving truck. He looked to the doc for clarification, but Doc's attention was on Ashley as he nodded with a smile. "Sounds like a good idea."

Once the door closed behind them and Blake knew Ashley would be out of earshot, he said, "What's this I hear about Ashley working alongside you?" Blake asked, a bit too rough with his approach. He'd never been good at confrontation. "And she has a moving truck coming?"

"They should've been here by now," Doc said, stepping out of the enclosed stall and latching the door behind him. Blake patiently waited for some kind of explanation of what had transpired without him knowing. "Drew and Garrett have fixed up the cabin on the east side of the property for her and Brycen to stay in for however long they need to—"

"Doc," Blake said, cutting him off mid sentence. Doc focused on Blake, waiting for him to say whatever it was he had to say. Blake paused long enough to get the words right before saying, "I can't afford to give up that cabin, and aside from what I've gathered here and there, I'm not even a hundred percent sure what she's doing here."

The old man nodded with a subtle grunt. "I figured that was the case. Drew and Garrett were overzealous with cleaning up the cottage and getting things prepared for my granddaughter's arrival."

"I mean," Blake said, "it's just not in the budget. It's been a hard year and with winter and calves coming... I'm not sure how—"

"I know," Doc said as he leaned against a sturdy post. "That's why I'm taking care of it. You don't have to worry about Ashley and Brycen for as long as they're here. I'll cover whatever they need."

Blake couldn't argue with that. If that's what Doc wanted to do, then so be it. But that still didn't answer why they were on the ranch. "What's going on, Doc?"

Doc offered a slight grin, but Blake could see the uncertainty in his eyes. The old man was pushing into his late seventies, and if Blake were to be honest, he'd thought about what he was going to do the day Doc retired and left the ranch.

"Ashley's had a hard go at things over the last two years, son," Doc said. "She's lost her husband, the father of her son, the love of her life…"

His words trailed off, leaving Blake to ponder how Brycen dealt with losing his father at such a young age. His heart went out to the boy, and he hadn't even met him yet. Just because Blake knew all about loss and growing up without a father.

"But anyway, she's been working on getting her degree in veterinary medicine and I can't help but help her achieve the one thing she's always wanted." Doc swiped a handkerchief out of the front pocket of his shirt and wiped the sweat from his brow. "Without getting into her business with you, I'll just say that I need her more than she'll ever need me. I might help her complete her internship while she's here, but I won't be around forever."

The man's words sank in as Blake listened. He knew the day would come when Doc wouldn't be able to continue his line of work at the ranch. For whatever reason, whether it be Blake's own selfish needs or whatever, he failed to believe it.

"So Ashley will live on the ranch with her son, Brycen, while assisting me and finishing up with her internship," Doc said matter-of-factly. "I've covered the cost of her schooling without hesitation because I know she'll be good for it. You won't have to worry about a thing while she's here. You just carry on with whatever you need to do for the ranch, and she and I will look after the livestock."

Blake thought about it for a minute. He thought about what that would mean as far as business went. He couldn't argue with it. It seemed like a win-win. He wouldn't have to pay her while running in the red as it was while she assisted Doc.

But there was one thing Blake needed to be clarified.

"How long's her internship?"

"A couple years," Doc stated.

Blake nodded as he pushed off the wood panel. "Alright. I suppose that isn't so bad."

Doc let out a light chuckle and clapped a hand on Blake's shoulder. "I'm sorry I didn't run things past you before bringing them here. I just figured it would all work out and keep everyone happy around here."

Blake gave the old man's shoulder a gentle squeeze and said, "I'd like to think I play a fair hand around here. I want everything to run as smoothly as it can."

Doc nodded in agreement, and a part of Blake ignored the realization that the old man was showing his age. He didn't want to think about the ranch running without Doc's help. The man had been a part of the ranch long before the Dixon brothers were even a thought in the back of their parents' mind. Doc had started out at the bottom of the totem pole and worked his way up to where he was now.

Blake glanced at his watch and tipped his hat back. "What do you say we go in and grab a bite to eat?"

Doc offered that familiar grin of his as Blake opened the door and stepped outside. The winds had picked up in the time they'd been in the barn, and yet another flurry of snowflakes was falling from the wide-open, gray-colored skies of Montana.

CHAPTER THREE

Ashley hadn't meant to overhear Blake as she exited the barn. If she could dismiss what she'd heard, she would in a heartbeat. She didn't want to know that Blake was upset about her being there. She thought her grandfather had okayed her moving to the ranch prior to insisting it was a good idea.

It had seemed too good to be true, and now she wasn't sure what to do next. She needed to call the moving company and find out where they were with her belongings. They should have arrived long before now.

She left the barn and headed toward the main house. Taking her time, she pulled her phone from the pocket of her jeans and dialed the number the owner of the moving company had given her.

No sooner had she hit the dial button than an older woman stepped onto the front porch. "Lunch is ready," she called out, flagging Ashley's attention from across the driveway. "You better come in and get yourself a plate before the boys. You know how grown men are with food."

Ashley smiled and said, "Thank you. I'll be right in."

With that, the older woman turned and headed back into the house. Ashley pressed the phone to her ear and waited for someone to pick up on the other end of the line. She'd learned patience over time and knew there had to be a good reason for the delay, but she couldn't help but worry something might have happened with her things.

"Good afternoon, thank you for calling—"

"Hi, this is Ashley Carlson," she politely interrupted. "I'm just checking to see where the movers are with my things? I haven't seen them, and I'm at the Dixon Ranch."

The man on the other end of the line tapped noisily on a keyboard as he typed something into the computer. Ashley waited as she made her way to the front porch. She knew everyone was gathering inside and grabbing their lunch, but the call should only take a few minutes. As soon as she knew where her stuff was and when it would get to the ranch, she would make her way inside.

"As far as I can tell, they'll be arriving within the next hour," the man said matter-of-factly. Ashley let out a relieved sigh. "I apologize. It has taken longer than expected. They experienced a delay early this morning."

Ashley knew all about delays. She had her own this morning as well. What with Brycen arguing about going to live on the ranch, and then avoiding a collision with the large red cow the ranchers called Big Red.

"Thank you," she said before ending the call. As long as Ashley knew their things would be there soon, she could relax. The last thing she needed to worry about was starting over without the few belongings she had left.

Ashley tucked her phone into her pocket and hesitated a minute before knocking on the door. The woman had invited her in, but knocking felt like the right thing to do.

The door creaked open and the same woman who had called out from the porch invited her in. "There's no need to knock around here," the woman stated. "Our house is your house."

Ashley smiled, thanking her for the invite once she stepped inside and followed the woman to the kitchen. A few familiar faces greeted her as she rounded the corner and walked past the long wooden table in the dining room. Garrett was sitting next to a woman with long blonde hair who looked to be around the same age, if not a few years younger, than Ashley. "Welcome to the ranch. I'm Shyann," the woman said with a smile and a friendly wave. Ashley smiled in return before following the older woman into the kitchen.

"We've known you were coming for some time now," the older woman said as she handed Ashley a plate of food. "Doc has told us all about you and your son, Brycen."

Ashley accepted the food with a soft "thank you" before moving from the kitchen and finding a spot to sit at the table. Everyone carried on with the conversation, agreeing that it was a long time coming and they were thankful to see that Doc had some help now.

"I suppose we should all introduce ourselves," the woman said, setting her fork down on her plate as she waited for the others to agree with her. "I'm Beverly Dixon, but you can call me Mama Dixon like the rest of them do around here."

Ashley smiled with a nod and said, "It's nice to meet you."

Several ranch hands introduced themselves, starting with Mason and ending with a few familiar faces she'd seen working outside.

"Becca will be here a bit later once Allie gets out of school," Drew said before taking a bite of food. Ashley wondered just how many women she would meet on the ranch, and if they were anything like her. She could only hope to make a few friends while she and Brycen were there. Even if it was only temporarily, she would try to make the best of it.

"Brycen's ten, right?" Drew asked, taking a drink and setting the glass back down in front of him.

"He just turned ten," Ashley said, thinking of the going-away birthday party they had for him. It had broken her heart to watch her son say goodbye one last time…

"I think he and Allie will get along just fine," Drew said, finishing the last of his food and sliding his chair away from the table. "She'll be happy to know she has someone to play with around here other than the animals."

Ashley offered a relieved smile. She would have been lying if she said she hadn't thought about Brycen's change when her grandfather talked them into moving to Woodford Creek. She was still up in the air about it, but she'd done a lot of praying and asked God to give her the guidance she needed, along with patience, to make the most out of the opportunity her grandfather had given her. "I'm sure Brycen will enjoy making a new friend as well."

With the sound of silverware scraping on the plates amid the silence, Shyann asked, "So you're a veterinarian, then? How long have you been practicing?"

Ashley swallowed her food, hardly prepared to answer their questions concerning her. "Well, I—"

The back door opened as Blake and her grandfather entered the house, saving her from further questioning as the others welcomed them to join in at the table.

"We'll get washed up and be right there," her grandfather announced. He found Ashley sitting in the crowd and offered her a comforting smile. She wasn't too sure what to expect after overhearing the first part of their conversation, but would make it a point to talk with her grandfather when they were alone. "We've worked up quite the appetite this morning."

She scooted her chair over, giving her grandfather plenty of room to squeeze in next to her. Thankfully, Blake had found a place to sit on the other end of the table. At least then she could judge his reactions according to the discussion if his brothers turned their attention back on her.

"Did you get a hold of the moving company?"

Blake's question caught her off guard as she took a drink of ice water. The ice clinked as she set the glass down in front of her. "I did," she replied. "They should be here any minute."

Blake nodded and went about eating his sandwich while the others continued on with the conversation.

"We made sure we got the cottage on the east side of the property ready once we heard you were coming," Mason said with a confident smile. Ashley looked across the table at Mason and thanked him for being so kind. He offered a shrug and said, "It's the least we could do. I have to admit it's good knowing Doc will have some help around here."

"Not that the old man can't handle things on his own," another younger ranch hand said, slapping her grandfather on the back.

Her grandfather gave a quick chuckle next to her as he finished the last bite of his sandwich. "Everyone's been fussin' over me for a while now," he said, addressing Ashley. Aside from his age, she wasn't sure what the fuss was all about. Her grandfather was a hardworking man, and no matter his age, she doubted his ability to work was all that affected. "I keep telling them I'm good as new, but they must think otherwise."

"That's not true at all," Mama Dixon said from the head of the table. "These boys just look out for one another around here. We all know you've got plenty of years left on the ranch. They just want to make sure they keep you on your toes, is all."

Ashley listened to the round of discussion as she finished the last of her lunch. It was good to know her grandfather was well taken care of at the ranch. The Dixon brothers and ranch hands seemed to admire him and his work ethic. She hoped they would welcome her just the same once she proved she could handle the job.

"So, Ashley," Mason said, "are you planning to stick around for the long haul?"

She felt Blake's eyes on her as he studied her, waiting for her to acknowledge Mason's question with an honest answer. "I'm here for as long as I'm needed."

Her grandfather patted her leg and offered a quick wink before saying, "She'll be finishing up her internship while learning a thing or two about ranch life. I will train her well enough so she can take over once I'm good and ready to retire."

Blake grunted at the other end of the table, causing the others to turn their attention toward him. He offered a quick wave of his hand as though he hadn't meant to interrupt the conversation. "Let's be honest, Doc," he said. "You'll never retire. Working on the ranch is in your blood. Too close to your heart to leave it all behind. Besides, you'd get bored real quick with nothing but time on your hands."

Her grandfather offered a subtle nod, but instead of agreeing with Blake, he said, "I've got plenty of things on my bucket list to keep me busy. I'd take up fishing on the lake in the mountains if I ran out of things to do."

A few of the ranch hands laughed and went along with him. Ashley couldn't help but wonder if her grandfather had already mentioned retiring a time or two. It seemed he had a plan for just about anything. If she were to be honest, he deserved retirement, but the thought made her nervous. She had a lot to learn before taking over for him.

"Well, hopefully you'll stick around here for a few more years before you wander off to the mountains in search of fish," Blake said, cracking a grin that caused her grandfather to smile.

"Trust me," her grandfather said, "you can't get rid of me that easily. I'll have plenty of time to chase fish when I get older."

Mama Dixon laughed as she scooted her chair back. "I'll tell ya… the cowpie is getting deep in here. I'll be washing the dishes if anyone needs me."

Ashley offered to help, but Mama Dixon told her to stay put and enjoy getting to know the others. "It won't take but a minute, anyway. I've got washing down pat over the years."

They watched Mama Dixon leave the dining room after helping her clear off the dirty dishes and placing them in the sink. Ashley wasn't used to sitting on her hands and not helping. She would make it a point to offer her help again at suppertime. It had to be tough keeping up with the household chores and feeding hungry grown men all day.

"She doesn't mind the dishes," Drew assured Ashley. "In fact, she enjoys keeping the house in order, don't you Ma?"

"Someone's gotta do it around here," Mama Dixon called out from the kitchen. "I'm just glad I have Becca to keep me sane while helping me out. I can thank Drew for that."

Ashley looked at Drew, waiting for an explanation, but was distracted by Blake's focus on her. There seemed to be something bothering him, but when she looked at him, he averted his attention elsewhere.

"Becca will be home with Allie here soon, and you can meet her then," Drew said, ignoring the passing glances between Ashley and Blake. Ashley nodded with a smile. She looked forward to not only meeting Becca, but her little girl as well. If the two of them were like the rest of the crowd, Ashley had no doubts she would like them.

"Well, it's time to get things done," Blake said, rounding up the ranch hands as he slid his chair back. "I've got to make a trip into town for a few things, but it shouldn't take too long."

His eyes landed on Ashley, causing her heart to skip a few beats. There was something about him that made Ashley wonder what he was thinking every time he looked at her. Was he still upset she was there at his ranch? Was he trying to come up with a way to tell her to leave?

"Garrett and Drew can help you get your things unloaded once the moving truck shows up," Blake stated, more like a command than an offer. There was no question who the boss was on the ranch. Not with the furrow in his brow or the firm tone in his voice as he looked at his brothers. "Once you're done helping her, you can get the cattle ready for tomorrow morning."

Ashley watched Blake leave the dining room. He grabbed his hat from the rack next to the door on his way out. She waited until he was out of earshot before asking her grandfather, "What's tomorrow?"

"Tomorrow's the day you'll learn all about tagging, branding, and vaccinating the cattle," he said with a slight grin. She couldn't deny the fact she was ready to learn. She did best with hands-on learning, but if she were to be honest, she was nervous.

As though her grandfather read her mind, he gave her leg a gentle pat and said, "It's now or never, Ash. I think you'll do just fine."

CHAPTER FOUR

Blake walked onto the front porch and slipped on his hat before reaching into the front pocket of his Wranglers for his truck keys. He needed to head into town for a few things at the co-op before it got too late in the afternoon.

With calving in process and a cold front moving in, he needed to make sure they stocked the cattle with plenty of feed. He planned to stock up on bags of cedar chips and other materials to ensure the cattle and their newborns stayed dry and warm.

"Mind if I ride along with you?" Doc called out from behind him.

Blake tore his attention from the far north corner of the property. He turned to face Doc as he stepped onto the porch with Ashley by his side. Blake couldn't help but catch a second glance at her before she politely excused herself and headed toward the barn.

"I don't mind," he said, watching Ashley walk off. "Where's she going?"

Doc stood in silence for a minute before answering Blake. "I believe she's heading to the barn to check on the calf and its mama."

Blake searched the property for any sign of his brothers. He thought he'd told them to stand by and wait for the moving truck, which hadn't arrived yet.

"Have you seen my brothers?"

"They're out in the pasture working on that fence line," Doc said, pointing toward the south pasture. Sure enough, Blake spotted his brothers mending yet another break in the fence line.

"I'm going to do something about that heifer," Blake grumbled as he walked down the porch steps. "She can't keep breaking out and wasting their time with repairs."

"Maybe you should check and see what other options there are for a stronger fence," Doc said with a light chuckle. Garrett had mentioned the same thing to Blake a couple of months back, but like everything else, it had to wait awhile. They couldn't replace something without money. Money made the world go 'round, and there was no telling how long they had before their world came to a complete halt.

As though Doc read his thoughts, he said, "I

wonder if you can find something cheaper by asking around. Maybe an old farmer is looking to get rid of some."

Blake didn't dismiss the old man's suggestion. It was a good idea to check around. Maybe he would talk to a few of the guys at the co-op and see if they knew of anyone looking to get rid of some material.

He climbed into the driver's seat of his old truck and motioned for Doc to hop into the passenger seat. As he pulled out of the driveway, a thought crossed his mind. The old Riggs farm next door that now belonged to his uncle Curt more than likely had some old fencing sitting around. Blake couldn't see how his uncle would find any use for it. Not right this minute, anyway.

Pulling out onto the highway, Blake guided the truck along the back roads as they headed into town. They would make the trip quick and maybe they would be back in time to oversee the unloading of the moving truck.

"Are you still mad?" Doc questioned as Blake steered the truck along the winding road.

Blake shot him a puzzled look. "Mad? I wasn't mad."

He could swear he hadn't been mad all he wanted to, but Doc knew him better than to believe that. Doc knew him better than anyone else on the ranch—other than his mother.

Blake tilted his head from side to side, feeling the heat from Doc's stare. "Okay," he said, offering a subtle grin. "I might've been a little worked up, but you have to understand—"

"I do," Doc said, adjusting the bill of his cap. "I know what it's like running in the red, son. I've been there a time or two myself."

Blake wasn't too sure of the point Doc was trying to make. He thought they'd put it behind them. They'd agreed as long as Blake didn't have to worry about paying her. Everything was kosher. Maybe not everything, but right now, as far as money was concerned. The last thing Blake wanted was to lose the ranch and fail at making his father proud.

"I can tell you're trying to figure everything out," Doc said. Blake shrugged. The old man couldn't blame him for trying to get a handle on things at the ranch. It took a lot of work to make sure everything was running smoothly. Even on bad days when he found kinks along the way, he tried his best to find a solution to the problem before it blew out of control. "You're not only wondering why I'd bring a city girl to the ranch, but you're also wondering what my plan is. Am I right?"

To say the old man hit the nail on the head would be an understatement. Blake wasn't sure how to respond to being called out like that. So instead, he answered with a subtle shrug as the muscles in the back of his neck tensed. He didn't like not knowing things. If it involved his ranch, his business, Blake had every right to know.

"I said nothing about her being a city girl," Blake stated, finally able to come back with something rather than staying quiet. "It almost seems like she's a fish out of water here, but I just don't know her, that's all."

"But you will," Doc said matter-of-factly. "Not everything has to be figured out right this minute, son. You don't have to know every detail in order to make things work. You've got to have a little faith and trust in others."

Blake disagreed, but nodded anyway. Trust was scarce. It was something that had to be earned. He'd been burnt too many times before. One time was too many. Even his own brother had figured that out the hard way when he'd left the ranch and came crawling back.

"All I'm sayin' is she's good for it," Doc said, resting his arm against the window. "Ashley and Brycen just need a little help to get back on their feet. And I believe the ranch is the best place for them to do just that."

Blake nodded as he turned off the highway and pulled into the lot next to the co-op. He shifted the truck into park and killed the engine before turning to face Doc. There was something the old man wasn't telling him, and it bugged him not to know what was going on. What the real reason was for bringing Ashley and her son to the ranch.

He had a bad feeling there was something going on with the veterinarian. Something he wasn't willing to share with Blake just yet. Something didn't feel right. Maybe Doc wanted Blake to just go along with it without asking questions, but that wasn't something he did.

"What's the reason you brought them to the ranch, Doc?"

His question pulled the man's wandering gaze away from whatever was happening outside of the truck as he turned to look at Blake. If Blake didn't know any better, Doc wanted to tell him the truth, but was having a hard time finding the words to say it.

"I've already told you why," Doc said, keeping his eyes locked on Blake's. "All you need to know is what I've already told you. You're thinking too much. There's nothing more to know. She's here to finish up her internship and earn her keep."

Blake knew better than to push the old man. He'd said all he was going to say, and there was nothing Blake could say or do to change that.

CHAPTER FIVE

Ashley walked out of the barn after checking on the calf and its mama. Both seemed to adjust well, but would still require additional TLC for a few days.

She watched as Blake and her grandfather climbed into Blake's truck and headed out onto the highway toward town. She wondered if her grandfather would make things right with Blake, so it wouldn't be so awkward between them.

She made her way down the driveway when the moving truck turned off the highway. Gravel crunched under the weight of the truck as the driver pulled in. She offered a friendly wave, trying her best to hide her frustration with its late arrival.

Drew and Garrett came up from the fence they had been working on to greet the driver of the moving truck. Before Ashley approached the truck, Drew and Garrett were directing the driver toward the east side of the property.

Ashley checked the time on her phone. In less than two hours, Brycen would ride the bus home from school. Home. She'd referred to the ranch as home a handful of times, but it hadn't hit her until now. She was starting over in a town she barely knew. On a ranch she knew nothing about. She had taken the advice from her grandfather, accepted the fact she needed to line Brycen up ahead of time to start school the same day they planned to move in. "Start him on the right foot, and he'll settle in with no problem," her grandfather had said. He seemed so certain that Ashley and Brycen would have no problem adjusting to life in Woodford Creek.

"Hey," Drew called out as he approached her on a four wheeler. "Hop on. We're heading to your place."

Without hesitation, Ashley climbed onto the four wheeler and held on the best she knew how as Drew guided them down the winding gravel driveway toward the place she would make a home for her and Brycen.

Once stopped, Ashley climbed off and stood back as the guys prepared to unload the moving truck. The driver apologized for arriving late, and Ashley accepted without hesitation. She knew things happened and there was no way to control everything.

She readied herself at the back of the truck, more than willing to help carry in the boxes and totes, but the Dixon brothers both shooed her away with a friendly "we've got this." She wasn't used to not helping get things done, but she wouldn't argue if they did the heavy lifting.

"If you'd like, you can go on inside and start directing where boxes go and getting things settled," Drew offered as he carried a large blue tote past her on his way into the cabin. Ashley accepted his offer and followed him inside.

The cabin was nothing like she envisioned it would be. For whatever reason, she'd thought it would be the bare minimum of a basic cabin. The wooden porch wrapped its way around the front half of the house, causing Ashley to imagine what the mornings would be like as she sat outside and drank coffee.

She stepped through the front door and was taken aback at first glance. The cottage appeared to be a little too small on the outside, which had caused her to think about how crowded she and Brycen would be while living there. Looks were deceiving as she took in the openness of the living space.

Near the front door, a built-in coat rack awaited her jacket and stocking hat, and she took them off and hung them on a hook. The guys moved around her, carrying in the furniture, boxes, and totes, and asking her where she would like them. She wasn't too picky about where to place them, so she pointed to the far corner of the spacious living room next to the fireplace.

"I'll bring some firewood from the shed once you get settled," Garrett said as Ashley admired the place she now called home. It was nothing like she imagined it would be. "With the cold front moving in, it's bound to get chilly here once the sun goes down."

She thanked him for being so kind. The Dixon brothers all seemed thoughtful in their own way, including Blake. Even though Blake seemed uncertain, she hoped he would come around and realize she wasn't a threat to the ranch.

"There you are," Drew called out, slapping his hands against his pant legs. He'd placed the kitchen table and chairs in the dining area and offered Ashley a thumbs up. "You'll have this place looking more like a home in no time."

Ashley smiled with a nod. She felt hopeful that everything would fall into place and she wouldn't regret her decision to move there. So far, it seemed like she'd made the right choice—no matter how concerned Blake seemed to be, she had faith that he would warm up to her grandfather's idea.

"Thanks again for all your help," she called out to the Dixon brothers as they climbed onto their four wheelers. Garrett tipped his hat with a subtle nod while Drew offered a quick wave before driving off down the gravel road that would lead them back to the main property.

She checked the time on her phone once again, counting down the minutes she had until Brycen would get off the bus. Everything was falling into place. She only hoped that Brycen had a good time at school making new friends before adjusting to their new life on the ranch.

Ashley worked on getting the totes and boxes unpacked according to the current room she was working in. She wanted to start with the living room, as that seemed to be the easiest. Thankfully, she had labeled the containers accordingly, so she didn't have to waste time searching for misplaced items.

She worked hard in the living room for at least thirty minutes. She was placing the afghan her grandmother had given her over the back of the couch when someone knocked on the front door and she heard a familiar voice call out, "Ashley?"

Ashley dropped what she was doing, excited to see Mama Dixon as she hurried to the door. When she opened the door, both Mama Dixon and Shyann greeted her with pies in hand.

"We figured we would bring a little something as a housewarming gift," Mama Dixon said, handing off the fresh-baked pie before shrugging out of her coat. "We weren't sure what kind of pie you and Brycen like, so we baked two. One is an apple, and the other is French silk chocolate."

Mama Dixon glanced over her shoulder with a sheepish smile. "Even though it's hardly anything to call it baking a chocolate pie."

Shyann shared a laugh with Ashley as she handed off the pie. Ashley carried them into the kitchen and set them on the counter. "Thank you, but you don't have to go out of the way for me."

"It's what we do best around here," Mama Dixon said, giving Ashley a gentle pat on her arm. "I figured it's the least we can do while you and your boy get settled in."

"Thanks again," Ashley said. "Would you like something to drink? I can dig my coffee pot out of one of these totes and get some coffee going."

Mama Dixon looked at Shyann, who offered a friendly shrug and accepted Ashley's offer. Ashley led them to the kitchen table, thankful the moving truck had brought it in time.

Mama Dixon paused near the table as she looked around. "Is there anything we can do to help you out? I'm sure the two of us can help unpack and get things settled."

Ashley politely declined her offer as she motioned for them to take a seat at the table.

Ashley pulled up a chair next to Mama Dixon and Shyann, more than ready to get to know them better.

She felt as though she belonged there—like she was right where she needed to be.

"First, I want to apologize for Blake," Mama Dixon said as the coffee pot grumbled to life in the kitchen behind them. Ashley wasn't sure what she was apologizing for. Blake had helped her out of the ditch and back onto the road. He might have seemed annoyed and frustrated once he realized she was there to stay, but she couldn't blame him. "Just give him some time. He'll relax and come around once he realizes you're not an extra worry added to the ranch."

"Why would he worry about me being here?" Ashley questioned, sliding out of her chair and making her way to the freshly brewed coffee. She dug three mugs out of a nearby container and poured each of them a steaming cup of coffee. Carrying them to the table, she said, "I'm just here to help my grandfather."

Mama Dixon shook her head and waved it off. "Oh, we know that, but—" Shyann interrupted, "Blake's always been protective of this ranch. Ever since he was little, he wanted to make his father proud. But he'll come around and warm up to the thought of having you around, eventually."

Ashley caught the gist of what Shyann was saying, but her mind took off in another direction. She hadn't met Blake's father yet. To be honest, she hadn't thought twice about not meeting him. She figured she would meet everyone on the ranch within time.

"I suppose we should stop chit-chatting and let you get back to unpacking," Mama Dixon said, finishing the last of her coffee and placing the empty cup in the sink. "We just wanted to stop by and welcome you home."

"Thank you. That means a lot to me," Ashley said, walking with both women to the front door. "You're welcome here anytime."

It seemed silly to welcome them to a place that belonged to them, but Ashley knew deep down that it was the polite thing to do. Mama Dixon turned and wrapped her arms around Ashley, giving her a warm hug that she hadn't realized she'd needed. "Let us know if there's anything you need, and just remember what I said about Blake. Give him some time. He'll come around."

Ashley smiled as she embraced the two women who welcomed her to the ranch with open arms and the hope of a blossoming friendship.

She waved one last time before closing the door and thanked God for the blessings in her life.

CHAPTER SIX

Blake pulled off the highway and headed down the driveway before parking the truck next to the woodshed. Garrett was swinging the ax as Blake and Doc stepped out of the truck and made their way over to him.

"We've got Ashley all settled in the cabin on the east side," Garrett announced, taking another swing against the block of wood in front of him. "I figured I'd get a bit more wood chopped before I take her some for the fireplace."

Blake nodded, appreciating his brother's dedication to doing the right thing.

"I plan to take a few bundles to her after a while," Garrett said, swinging the ax over his shoulder and splitting the wood. He was a pro at splitting wood, and Blake appreciated his brother's effort to keep the woodshed stocked for the upcoming winter months.

"I can do that if you've got other things to do," Blake said, taking both his brother and Doc by surprise. Doc grinned and gave Blake a knowing look, but Blake ignored it.

"Alright," Garrett said, "I'll let ya do that while I tend to the cattle. I still have a list of things to scratch off before the sun goes down."

"How'd the fence turn out?" Blake hadn't thought to check the fence when he first pulled in. Garrett was good at fixing things around the ranch. There was no doubt he couldn't handle repairing the fence.

"It'll do for now," Garrett said with a slight shrug. "Not much more that old fence can take, though. We'll have to figure out something real quick if we want to keep the predators out of the pastures."

Blake nodded in agreement. It had been a long time coming with that fence. He'd put it off long enough and now he risked paying for it when the wolves and mountain lions roamed the property line.

"If you've got an extra minute or two this evening, how about checking with Curt? See if he has anything lying around on that old property of his that he might part with."

Garrett set the ax down, leaning it against the side of the woodshed, before agreeing to Blake's request. "I can head over there now. Catch him before it gets too late," Garrett said, adjusting his cowboy hat and stepping over a pile of chopped wood. "Maybe then I'll still have time to take what he gives us and make it work."

Blake slapped a hand on his brother's shoulder, happy to know he would drop what he was doing to help at any minute. Running a ranch was a team effort. Blake liked to think he ran a tight ship, and he was proud of it.

"I'm going to head to the barn and check on the calf and its mama," Doc said, combing a hand through his gray hair and placing the ball cap back on his head. "I want to make sure the calf is staying warm enough and that her mama is giving her the attention she deserves."

Blake checked the time on his watch and realized the kids would get off the bus within the next half hour. He couldn't help but wonder about Ashley's son, which made him question what their full story was yet again.

Shrugging it off, he pulled a bundle of wood together, stacking it up in the back of his truck. He would take at least a half-bed full of wood to Ashley's cabin. If he were to be honest, it would give him a chance to apologize for appearing a jerk. His talk with Doc made him question everything, including his need to control it all. There were some things out of his control. He would agree with that. But, then again, it was just who he was, and so far he had a lot to show for it.

Placing the last of the wood in the back of the truck, he closed the tailgate and climbed into the driver's seat. He fired up the old truck and backed out of the spot he'd taken next to the shed. As he shifted the truck into drive, he experienced a moment of hesitation. What if she didn't want him there? What if she didn't accept his apology and realize that, deep down, he was a nice guy? His need for control over the ranch had little to do with the size of his heart. He would do anything for anyone in a time of need...

Then why was he having such a hard time accepting the fact that Ashley would live on the ranch for the next few years?

Shrugging off the nagging guilt, Blake trundled the truck down the gravel road toward the east side of the property. The cabin sat off in the distance, a bit out of sight of the main house. It would give Ashley and her son plenty of space to live with no one invading their privacy.

Blake parked near the front porch and killed the engine before climbing out of the truck. It was now or never, and he prefered to get the tough stuff out of the way. He glanced toward the front door, wondering if he would interrupt Ashley as she settled in. Shaking his head, he unlatched the tailgate and slipped on a pair of worn leather gloves. He was a grown man and wasn't too proud to make things right.

As he reached into the back of the truck and grabbed a pile of wood, he heard footsteps on the front porch behind him. He set the wood down next to the makeshift woodshed and turned to face the woman he came to apologize to.

He tipped his hat out of habit, feeling nervous now that she was standing on the front porch watching him. "I figured I'd bring out some wood for the fireplace."

Usually, he was more for talking, but somehow he managed to only stammer over his words as he struggled to figure out what to say. She stood motionless on the wooden front steps, trying to figure out why he wasn't being a jerk. He hated that first impressions lingered for so long. It didn't count that he'd pulled her out of the ditch. Not when he turned around and questioned her arrival.

"Thank you," she said in a soft voice. If he hadn't been staring at her, he would have missed she'd said anything at all. "Garrett said I'd need that with the cold front moving in."

Blake didn't care to talk about the weather, but he had to let her know his brother was right. It could get downright cold out here in the mountains of Montana. Something he assumed she wasn't used to in the city.

He grabbed a few more armfuls of wood and stacked them among the rest.

He focused on unloading the wood, and hadn't realized Ashley had made her way down the porch steps and was now standing beside his truck.

"I'm sorry that you were the last to know about us moving here," she said, her voice soft and filled with concern. He hated himself for making her feel unwelcome. That had never been his intention. "I just figured Gramps had everything all planned out and everyone would be aware of our arrival."

He felt gutted by her words. They wouldn't have affected him so much if he hadn't realized she must have overheard his conversation with Doc. How could he have been so careless with his words while knowing she could have been standing right outside the barn?

"You don't have to apologize, Ash," he said, shortening her name a little too naturally. "I should be the one saying how sorry I am for acting so irrational. I had no reason to question your grandfather's decision. If he feels it's what's best for the ranch," he quickly added, "and you, then I should've kept my mouth shut and went along with it."

Ashley shook her head, making him question if she wasn't accepting his apology. "I can't say that I wouldn't have done the same thing if someone brought a stranger onto my land and threatened my livelihood."

He quirked a brow at the mention of a threat. Had he given her the impression that he felt threatened?

Blake slipped off his gloves and hat before running a quick hand through his hair. He couldn't argue with the fact that his instincts had kicked in, but he didn't see Ashley as a threat… not even once since he'd first met her.

"I just have a lot to look after around here," Blake said, keeping his eye on her as she leaned against his truck. Her long blonde hair fell evenly over the blanket draped around her shoulders. He looked down and realized she was standing in the snow with only a pair of house slippers on her feet. "You should probably go inside before you freeze in those things."

Ashley stuck a foot in the air and wiggled it. "These? Slippers, you mean?"

He chuckled off the embarrassment of not finding the right words. There was something about her that caused him to lack an intelligible sentence. "I know what they are. I just couldn't think—"

The sound of pattering footfalls on the path behind them interrupted him mid sentence. A younger boy ran alongside Allie as they raced toward the cabin. "I'll get there first," Allie called out behind her. The boy, Blake assumed to be Brycen, was doing his best to keep up with Allie as she approached what she declared "home base".

"Uncle Blake," Allie called out, wrapping her arms around his waist. "I met a new friend on the way home."

Brycen stopped running once he hit home base and bent over as he rested his hands on his knees. "His name is Brycen, and he's going to live here," Allie announced, backtracking and grabbing Brycen's arm. She guided him back to where Blake and Ashley were standing with a big smile on her face. "Is that true?"

Blake turned to Ashley, who was nodding her head with a smile. "It is."

Allie looked from Blake back to Ashley and said, "You must be Brycen's mama?"

Ashley stepped forward, kneeling down to meet the little girl with an outstretched hand. "I am. My name is Ashley," she said with a smile. "You must be Allie?"

Allie nodded enthusiastically with a proud smile. "I am!"

"I've heard a lot about you. It's nice to meet you," Ashley said, looking back over her shoulder at Blake. He certainly hadn't thought seeing her interact with his niece would do much, but he hated to admit it might have warmed his heart a little.

"Ashley's the new veterinarian here at the ranch,"

Blake said, noticing a slight tension in Ashley when he mentioned it. "She'll be working alongside Doc while she finishes up with her schooling."

Allie furrowed her brow. "School? You go to school, too?"

Brycen quipped, "No, she doesn't go to school. Not like we do anyway."

"Well, something like yours, except for grownups," Ashley explained. Blake relaxed his shoulders as he leaned back against his truck. "I'm not quite finished, but once I do, I'll have my degree in veterinary medicine."

Allie looked at Blake for clarification, but it was all news to Blake. He did not know Ashley wasn't a certified veterinarian. The way Doc had talked, she was already practicing as a vet and just finishing out her internship for a greater degree. But then again, maybe Blake just misunderstood yet again. He didn't know how that all worked. But if he were to be honest, it kind of bothered him a bit that she wasn't who he thought she was. If she was going to be working alongside Doc, learning a thing or two about the ranch and Blake's livestock, he would have thought she'd have some experience with animals...

"Brycen, this is my uncle Blake," Allie said, pulling Blake from his thoughts. "He runs the ranch."

Blake nodded as his niece introduced them. He

shook Brycen's hand in a way a man shook a younger man's hand while patting him on the arm.

"He's the boss," Allie whispered, leaning close to Brycen's ear and blocking her mouth with her hand. "What he says goes around here."

Blake let out a loud laugh as he adjusted his hat. He couldn't deny it made him feel good being introduced like that, but he didn't want Allie to scare the poor kid and make him afraid of him.

"I might be the boss, but I'm not a bad guy," Blake said, trying his best to convince the kid otherwise. "I might lay down the rules around here, but I'd like to think I'm pretty easy going."

Ashley's snicker caught him off guard. He whipped around and quirked a brow. She'd just met him. What did she know about him, aside from the fool he'd made of himself?

"Come on," Allie said, tugging on Brycen's arm once again. "Nana always has cookies waiting for me after school."

Brycen glanced at his mother as Blake moved off to the side. He needed to wrap things up and head back down to the barn. There were a few things he needed to finish up to prepare for tomorrow's big event.

Ashley gave her son a quick nod, letting him know it was okay to go along with Allie. It was good to see that she was comfortable letting her son get to know the ranch without her. Blake would let Brycen know a few rules regarding the bullpens and keeping his distance from the other livestock on the ranch. He didn't want to worry about anyone getting hurt by the large herds. And he especially didn't want it to be a young kid who wouldn't know any better.

After watching the kids race off, Blake latched the tailgate and made his way to the driver's side. He opened the door and tossed his gloves into the cab of his truck. He turned to face Ashley, but she had already made her way back to the porch.

"This should keep you warm for a while," Blake stated, pointing at the stack of wood he'd placed next to the front porch. "I will keep it stocked so you don't run out."

Ashley nodded and pulled the blanket tighter around her shoulders. Assuming it was best that he let her get back inside and out of the cold, Blake gave a quick wave and climbed into his truck.

She stood on the landing and offered a soft smile. "Thanks for stopping by," she called out with a wave. Before turning to head inside, she stopped and said, "And Blake…"

He held the door open long enough to hear what she had to say.

"I accept your apology."

Blake nodded with a grin as he shut the door and fired up the truck. He watched as she turned and headed inside. He couldn't help listing all the reasons it wouldn't be good to get too close to Ashley Carlson. She wouldn't be on the ranch all that long. Once she got a taste of what life on the ranch was all about, she'd be hightailing it back to the city by winter's end.

CHAPTER SEVEN

Ashley watched Blake drive off and thought about the way he looked at her. She appreciated his thoughtfulness, making sure she had plenty of wood to keep them warm. Truthfully, his random act of kindness surprised her. She hadn't expected him to be the one following up on his brothers' word to get her settled in.

But then again, it made perfect sense. Blake was the boss of the ranch. Of course, he would take it upon himself to make sure everything was taken care of. He couldn't help double-checking his brothers' words and making sure they'd done what they'd said.

Ashley walked over to the fireplace and placed two more logs into the fire she'd started prior to Blake's arrival. She grabbed the afghan she'd draped over the back of the couch and sat down in the chair next to the fire.

She thought about the conversation she'd overheard. Blake had seemed to be worried about the books and keeping up with payroll. She couldn't help but wonder how far in the red the Dixon Ranch was running while thanking God her grandfather had been willing to cover the cost of living while she and Brycen were there at the ranch.

Losing her husband had turned their world upside down and inside out. The medical bills for his cancer treatments ate away at their life savings, something neither of them could have planned for. Soon after her husband's diagnosis, Ashley had no choice but to pause her schooling and focus on taking care of him while doing her best with making ends meet.

Her thoughts drifted to a time when she was happy as she watched the flicker of the flames. A time long before cancer threatened to take away the one person who meant the most to her. The love of her life. The one who encouraged her to chase her dreams while giving her the best of everything.

Footsteps on the front porch pulled Ashley from her thoughts as she stood from the chair. The front door opened and Brycen rushed inside. His cheeks were rosy red and his brown hair peeked out from the edge of his stocking hat.

"Mom, guess what?" he called out as he kicked off his winter boots and shoved them to the side.

"What?" Ashley asked, wiping away a few stray tears.

"Mama Dixon said that we're invited for supper tonight," Brycen announced as he met Ashley with a hug. "And grandpa said I can see the calf after we're done eating."

"Is that right?"

"Allie showed me where the calving barn is and everything," Brycen said, smiling up at her with bright blue eyes. "Blake said I'm not allowed to go anywhere near the animals. But Allie and Drew showed me the horses and told me they would give me riding lessons as long as you say it's okay."

Ashley thought about it for a minute before saying, "I'm okay with that as long as your homework is done and you're extra careful."

"I will be. I promise."

Brycen wrapped his arms around her, offering her a quick hug before racing off. She watched as he explored the cabin, taking in the view from the large bay window in the living room. A view of the mountains in the distance was something she could get used to.

As he bounded up the stairs to the loft where she'd set up his room, he said, "This place is awesome!"

His excitement was contagious, and Ashley couldn't thank God enough for answering her prayers. She'd been worried about the change. Whether Brycen would enjoy living on the ranch after saying goodbye to his friends in the city. She had dreaded the move in fear that he wouldn't like it there.

"Gramps says that you're going to help him tomorrow while I'm at school," Brycen said as he walked down the stairs. "Will I be able to help after school?"

"I'm not sure," Ashley said, not a hundred percent certain there would be anything for her ten-year-old son to accompany them with. "I guess we'll have to wait and see."

Brycen walked around the cabin and talked about how happy he was to be there. Life on the ranch seemed so cool, and he couldn't wait to learn all about the animals. Ashley listened contentedly as her son mentioned the list of things Allie showed him. She felt relieved knowing he was settling in and seemed to adjust fine.

"Let's go," Brycen said, excitement bounding in his voice as he tugged on Ashley's arm. "I want to see everyone. Allie says Mama Dixon makes the best suppers ever."

Ashley allowed the boy's excitement to carry her to the door. He barely gave her enough time to slip on her shoes before bounding out the door and down the front porch steps.

"Wait for me, please," she called after him from the landing.

Brycen stopped at the edge of the sidewalk and waited for her to catch up to him. Ashley draped an arm over her son's shoulders and walked along the winding gravel road toward the main house. It was their first day on the ranch and they'd been welcomed with open arms—something she would be forever grateful for.

A few short minutes later, they were climbing the front porch steps of Mama Dixon's house. She could hear loud talking intermittently, interrupted by rounds of laughter. Suppers at the Dixon house seemed to be the highlight of everyone's night if the joy coming from inside the house was any sign.

Brycen stood beside her and waited as she knocked on the door. She smiled down at Brycen, trying her best to hide how nervous she felt. She wasn't used to big gatherings. It had been just her and Brycen for the last two years, with an occasional visit from good friends. Nothing extravagant, like what she imagined awaited them on the other side of the door.

They were greeted by a smiling woman Ashley hadn't met yet, but she was certain it had to be Becca. Her brown hair fell to her shoulders in perfect curls and, if Ashley had to guess, she wasn't too much younger than her. Everyone at the ranch seemed to be in their late twenties to early thirties. It was comforting to know she was among several in her age group.

"Come on in," the woman said, taking Brycen's coat and hanging it on an unoccupied hook near the door. Where there wasn't a coat, there was a cowboy hat. Ashley found a vacant spot and hung her coat, stuffing her hat and gloves into an empty pocket. "You must be Ashley?"

Ashley smiled and accepted the woman's outstretched hand in front of her. "It's so nice to meet you. I've heard so much about you already."

Ashley nodded with a smile. "Becca, right?"

"Yes," Becca said. "I'm Allie's mother. Let me tell you... She's talked nonstop about you and Brycen since the two of them got off the bus."

Ashley smiled down at Brycen, who looked up at her and offered a silly shrug. "Girls," was his only response before being dragged away from the door by an overly excited Allie. He tossed a look back at Ashley as if to say, "See what I mean?"

Becca waved them off, reminding them not to run inside. She turned her attention back to Ashley and said, "I would've stopped over earlier, but Mama Dixon needed a few things from the grocery store for supper."

"No worries at all," Ashley assured her. "I've been unpacking and getting everything settled."

Becca offered a warm smile. "I know how all that goes. Allie and I have moved a few times," she stated, glancing over her shoulder and checking on the children. "But I think we've finally found a place to call home now."

Becca quickly dismissed their conversation and stepped away from the door. "Enough chit-chatting, let's join the others. There will be plenty of time to get to know each other."

Ashley followed her into the dining room and stopped in her tracks as soon as her eyes landed on Blake. He was sitting next to an empty chair and motioned for her to sit down. Her heart skipped a beat as she hesitated, but soon realized it was the only available spot. She couldn't refuse his offer.

She walked around the oblong table and was surprised when Blake stood and pulled her chair out.

"You didn't have to do that," she whispered to him as she sat down.

He leaned over and whispered, "I know it's hard to believe, but I'm a gentleman. Besides, have you ever seen Ma crack a whip?"

Ashley snuck in a quick glance at Mama Dixon. She was standing at the other end of the table, giving Blake a knowing look. A part of Ashley found it hard to believe that Mama Dixon would have a tough love side to her, but then again, she raised three boys. Ashley sometimes had her hands full with just one.

"My boys better always be on their best behavior, or else," Mama Dixon said, slapping a wooden spoon against her palm. The table cracked with laughter, but Ashley knew better than to think the woman was joking. "Now, who's ready to eat?"

Several "yes, ma'am's" rounded the table, and Mama Dixon offered a proud smile. They called Allie and Brycen to join them at the table once they washed up. It didn't take the two of them long before they were climbing into chairs next to Becca and Ashley.

"Can I say grace?" Allie asked, folding her hands in front of her and waiting for the go ahead.

Mama Dixon nodded once and Allie started, "Dear Father, we thank you for the food on our table and for Nana. Thank you for allowing us time to spend together."

"A—"

"Wait," Allie called out, stopping everyone from finishing grace with an amen. "I wasn't done yet."

Everyone settled back with their hands still folded in front of them and waited for Allie to say her last words of grace.

"I also want to thank you for bringing Ashley and Brycen to the ranch. I really like them."

Allie's words melted Ashley's heart. She'd heard

plenty of grace spoken at meals, but never had one affected her the way Allie's had.

"Amen," Allie stated, sliding back in her chair and smiling over at Ashley.

Several "amens" rounded the table, and Ashley couldn't help but whisper "thank you" to the little blonde-haired girl sitting across from her.

Blake handed her a bowl of mashed potatoes, followed by green beans. When he tried to pass her the plate of grilled cheeseburgers, she kindly refused his offer. She hadn't eaten meat since she was a teenager—a time when she was determined to become a vegetarian.

He raised a brow, questioning her, or maybe he was looking at her like she'd grown a second head. Either way, she passed the plate to Brycen, who accepted a cheeseburger and placed it on his open bun.

"Wait a minute," Blake said, pointing at Brycen's plate as he looked at Ashley. "You don't eat meat?"

Ashley shook her head and realized the rest of the table was now looking at her. She hadn't thought it a big deal if she turned down meat, but she must have thought wrong. Of course, she was living on a ranch with Angus beef cattle in the pasture, but she hadn't thought twice about what the Dixon's would think.

Mama Dixon slid her chair back, standing from the table. "Is there anything else I can get for you? We have plenty of food in the fridge," she said, offering Ashley a sympathetic look. "I can put together something real quick if you'd like."

Ashley glanced around the table and found her grandfather giving her a reassuring smile. Just with one look, her grandfather was telling her it wasn't as big of a deal as Blake was making it out to be. It might not have been, but she still didn't want Mama Dixon cooking something different just for her. Ashley didn't need special treatment. She would find something to eat at home later if she was still hungry.

"No, thank you," Ashley said, relieved when Mama Dixon sat back down in her chair. "I'm fine with what I have here on my plate."

"Well, if you want something more, you just let me know," Mama Dixon said in a motherly voice that made Ashley miss her own mother.

Blake was still trying to figure her out once everyone started eating. Ashley furrowed a brow and whispered, "What?"

She didn't need anymore attention on her. She hated being the center of attention. Wasn't it bad enough already that his mother offered to cook something different just to accommodate her?

Blake shook his head but said nothing. At least not until he took a bite of his cheeseburger and swallowed it down with a sip of soda. "I thought you said you were a veterinarian, not a vegetarian. I must have heard you wrong."

Ashley mixed a forkful of butter into her mashed potatoes, trying her best to ignore Blake's comment. There was no doubt he'd picked up the fact she wasn't a certified veterinarian while talking with the kids after school. Now he was just being difficult about it.

"I don't see why a person can't be both," Mama Dixon stated as a warning to Blake to cut it out before changing the subject. "So, tomorrow's the big day, or so I hear?"

Blake grumbled something inaudible under his breath as he stabbed his fork into a stack of green beans.

"Ashley and I will spend most of the morning in the calving barn. We'll tag the newborn calf and get vaccinations lined up while the boys are busy roping and leading the rest of the cattle through the chutes," Ashley's grandfather said, taking a quick bite of food. "I have a feeling a few of those cattle won't be too happy by the time they get to us, so we'll be good and ready."

Ashley wasn't too sure what her grandfather was talking about. She hadn't spent too much time with him to get a good enough idea of what to expect at tomorrow's event. Not to mention it was her first time working up close and personal with livestock. She had a lot to learn in the little time her grandfather was giving her.

Blake cleared his throat and said, "I'd like for her to see the entire process."

Ashley swallowed hard and held her breath at the tone in Blake's voice. Was he really that upset that she didn't like eating meat? If that was the case, then he could just say so and be done with it. Wasn't it her grandfather who needed to be the one to show her the ropes around the ranch?

"I just think it'd be good for her to see it from the beginning to the end," Blake stated.

He was watching Ashley now, waiting for her to say it wasn't a good idea, but instead, she responded, "I'm okay with it as long as Gramps is."

She wasn't sure what to expect, but she supposed if she was going to learn a thing or two about the ranch, and live there for the foreseeable future, it was now or never.

CHAPTER EIGHT

The morning sun peeked through the mountains on the east side of the Dixon property line as Blake made his way to the calving barn. He would meet with the ranch hands after he checked in with Doc.

"Hey, Doc," Blake greeted as he slapped a hand on the old man's shoulder. "How're they doing?"

Doc fumbled an ear tag between his fingers before dropping it on the straw covered floor. He bent over to pick it up, but seemed to lose his balance. Blake reached out and grabbed Doc's elbow, steadying him as he waited for him to get his bearings.

"You alright, old man?" Blake asked, concerned about the sudden spell. It wasn't like Doc to lose his balance. "How about you sit down over here for a minute?"

Blake guided him to a nearby chair and helped him into it. He watched him closely, prepared for another spell to come. He studied Doc for a minute before asking, "What's going on, Doc?"

Doc looked at him with a puzzled look just as the door opened and Ashley stepped inside. She was bundled head to toe in warm winter gear, her brown hair falling in waves over her shoulders.

She looked from Blake to Doc and asked, "What's going on? Is everything alright?"

Blake tried to explain what he'd witnessed, but Doc interrupted him. "I'm fine. I just needed a minute."

The old man was tough as nails. There was no doubt about that. But in all the years Doc had worked on the ranch, Blake had never been as concerned about the old man as he was now. Something wasn't right.

"Gramps," Ashley said as she approached her grandfather's side. "Are you—"

"I'm fine," Doc stated, shrugging her off. "I just misstepped, is all, and lost my balance for a second there. Quit fussin' over me."

Blake met Ashley's concerned eyes and offered a slight shrug. If Doc said he was fine, Blake had no choice but to believe him. But that didn't mean he would leave the old man unattended anytime soon.

"I'm going to round up the ranch hands," Blake

said. "Ash, why don't you stay and help Doc get things ready with the tags and vaccines?"

The last thing he needed was for something to happen to Doc when no one was around to help him. His original plan of taking Ashley along with him for the day went out the window the minute Doc lost his balance.

"I'm fine," Doc said, trying his best to convince them. "You wanted to take her along—"

"Until I realized it was a foolish idea," Blake interrupted. "She doesn't need to be out there with me before she learns a thing or two from you. She'll have plenty of time to see how the system works. We'll do it again in the spring anyhow."

If Blake didn't know any better, Ashley seemed to relax a bit at the free pass. Had she not wanted to spend time with him? Was he really all that bad?

"Just remember, the white tags are for the bulls and the yellow are for heifers," Blake said to Ashley, making sure she understood. "And make sure the calves get the same number as their cow."

With a quick nod, she said, "Got it. White tag for bulls. Yellow tag for heifers. Mother and children have matching numbers."

"I think he was in the process of tagging the newborn calf with its mama's number before…"

Blake's words trailed off. The last thing he wanted

to do was upset Doc by mentioning the episode—whatever it was called, it hadn't been good.

"Got it," Ashley said, offering Doc a hand up as he scooted to the edge of the chair. Blake stood by for a minute, making sure Doc was okay to stand on his own before looking over at Ashley. "If you need me, I won't be too far. You've got your phone on you just in case?"

Ashley patted the pocket of her coat and said, "Always."

"Alright, Doc, be sure to teach her a thing or two," Blake teased as he slapped the man on the back. "I'll be back to check on things in an hour. There are plenty of heifers waiting on their tags and vaccines."

"We'll get them covered," Doc assured, offering Blake a small grin.

Ashley offered a subtle shrug when Blake looked at her, and he couldn't help but acknowledge the sudden need he felt to stick around. He didn't want to leave her and Doc unattended, but he had little choice if he was going to help round up the cattle and lead them through the gated chutes.

Doc and Ashley stood at the makeshift counter, sorting tags and arranging them by number as Blake made his way out of the barn. He didn't enjoy leaving them, but Doc seemed fine now. Maybe he just tripped, and that caused the old man to lose his balance. Blake hadn't paid too close attention until the man had nearly fallen into the wood paneling of the stall.

Climbing onto Chance, the black horse Drew had tamed, Blake set out toward the south pasture. He and Garrett spent most of the morning herding the cattle toward the gates and through the chutes. Mason and a few others readied the electric branding irons and scored the backend of several cattle and calves with a DBR before turning them loose.

Blake and Garrett did their best to separate the young bulls from the heifers to make tagging easier. The process from start to finish took only a day, but with the late start they had, there was a slight chance they would have to finish up tomorrow.

The clanking of metal gates and hooves echoed across the open pasture. Garrett rode alongside Blake, directing their two Australian Shepherds, the Wranglin' Duo, with quick commands.

"Do you think she's going to stick around?"

Garrett's question pulled Blake's attention from the rounding of cattle. Blake hesitated a moment, wanting to keep his focus on business. He'd thought about what Garrett was asking a time or two since meeting Ashley, but he wasn't good at reading people.

"As far as I know, she's here for a while," Blake said, circling back and rounding a few stragglers toward the gate. Garrett shook his head and gave the dogs another quick command before saying, "That's not what I asked."

Garrett had been the shy one of the three brothers. Blake could count on him to keep things private, unlike with Drew. Garrett was two years younger than Blake and was more or less his right-hand man when he needed him to be.

"I know what you asked," Blake said, riding alongside Garrett on their way back out to the pasture. "I'm not sure what to think."

Garrett whistled for the dogs to change direction, leading the cattle toward the gate once again. "Supper got a little intense, didn't it?"

Blake shrugged. He hadn't meant for it to. It had just caught him by surprise. "Because she's a vegetarian?"

Garrett shrugged, pulling on the reins and keeping the horse at a slow and steady pace. "I guess I just don't see what the big deal is. I mean, if Shyann didn't like eating meat, I wouldn't call her out for it."

Blake thought about it for a minute. He hadn't meant to cause a scene in front of everyone. He also hadn't expected a woman living on a ranch to turn down a cheeseburger. Was it silly of him to draw attention to it? Sure, but he'd meant no harm. He'd only been teasing her for Pete's sake.

"Do you see what I see?" Blake asked, changing direction in the conversation as he pointed off in the distance. "Those heifers are looking a bit rough if you ask me."

Garrett pulled back on his reins as Blake studied the herd. He didn't like the look of them. The last few weeks were hard, but they shouldn't be losing weight and looking as unsettled as they were. "I've noticed that over the last few days. What do you think is causing them to lose weight?"

Blake scanned the property line while looking for a sign of predators. They'd seen their fair share of mountain cats and bears in the woods surrounding the ranch, and it wasn't uncommon for wolves to make their presence known in the winter months, either, though it wasn't winter yet despite the bit of snow they already had.

"They're not settling because something's got them riled up," Blake said, taking hold of Chance's reins and guiding him toward the far end of the pasture. "You keep herding the cattle," he called out to Garrett. "I'm going to check on a few things."

Garrett adjusted his cowboy hat and offered a quick nod as Blake trotted toward the edge of the property. He didn't appreciate knowing his herd was losing weight and feeling unsettled. It made him uneasy knowing there was a threat to the ranch.

He had enough ranch hands to monitor the place, but even then, no one could watch the place twenty-four seven. It just wasn't possible.

Blake trotted along the property line, looking for breaks in the fence line and making sure there weren't gaps in the barbed wire. One day, they could replace the fencing with something more durable, more secure, that would keep their herds safe from the predators of the land.

He hadn't looked at the books in over a week, but he knew the ranch needed the cattle to keep their weight if there was a chance they'd succeed in today's market. Blake couldn't risk taking chances, what with running in the red while praying for some kind of miracle. He couldn't afford to keep the ranch, but he couldn't afford to lose it, either.

Once he inspected the fence line, he headed back to where he'd left Garrett. He would talk with his brothers and make sure they understood the threat the ranch faced. If he could get them on board with moving the cattle to a pasture closer to the main property, they would have a better chance at protecting them from the lurkers.

"Did you find anything?" Garrett asked, guiding the cattle toward the main gate and into the chute. "It wouldn't surprise me if there were wolves running along that fence line at night."

"That's what I'm afraid of," Blake said, rounding up the few stragglers left out of the last bunch. "If that's what's got them so unsettled, we're going to do our best to keep them close and protected while making sure we give them extra feed. We can't risk them losing too much weight, or we'll take a loss come spring."

Blake adjusted his hat, pulling it down over his eyes to block out the mid-morning sun as they drove the cattle east. "And we won't make a dime if the wolves attack the herd."

Blake had talked little with his brothers about the books. He didn't want to cause alarm when he was working on figuring it out. It might be something as simple as an overpayment that hadn't been documented correctly, or perhaps at all. He hadn't realized the woman they'd hired to look after the ranch's accounts hadn't known her head from her tail.

Blake just needed to find the time to sit down and go through the numbers with a fine-toothed comb. He was determined to find something amiss, and he could only pray it would be an easy fix. He'd thought about running it past Curt if he struggled to find what went wrong. His uncle would have a good idea what to look for since the ranch once belonged to him before he'd passed it on to the Dixon brothers.

"If you want, Mason and I can keep watch over the herd tonight," Garrett offered. "It wouldn't hurt to get some trail cams—"

"Not much good those would do after the fact," Blake stated matter-of-factly. Trail cams were a nice accessory, but that wouldn't help them protect their herd from being attacked by the nightly prowlers. Whether it was mountain lions or wolves, Blake knew the threat was high. "I guess it wouldn't hurt to have you and Mason watching over things. I think it'd be best if we alternate shifts throughout the night until I figure something out."

Garrett gave him a quick nod. "Sounds good. I'll let Mason know that we've got first watch tonight."

"I'm sure whatever's roaming the property line is here for the calves," Blake said. "The calves are easy targets if their cows aren't enough to protect them."

Blake thought about the newborn calf in the calving barn. They were expecting a few more mamas to deliver any day. He would mention something to Doc and Ashley about keeping a close eye on the birthing process. They would need to work together in order to get the birthing cows into the barn before delivering their calves. He couldn't risk having newborn calves in the pasture.

"So," Garrett said, pulling Blake's attention from his never ending to-do list. "You've never said what your thoughts are about Ashley. I mean, we all know you're upset that she's here and—"

"I'm not upset that she's here," Blake interrupted, shooting his brother a furrowed brow.

Garrett raised his hands in defense and laughed it off. "Easy, killer. I'm just curious to know what you're thinking. Just light conversation to carry us through the day, that's all."

"Well, I'm not upset that she's here," Blake repeated. He might have been a little cross when he'd first realized she would work alongside Doc, but that hadn't bothered him as much as not knowing. "She and Brycen will be a great addition to the ranch. And to be honest, no matter how many times Doc has told me he's fine…"

Garrett shot him a concerned look, and Blake shook his head. "He's fine. I just think it'll do him some good to have Ashley around. Maybe once she learns a thing or two, Doc can take some time off."

Blake didn't want to cause concern where it wasn't needed. He would make it a point to talk to Ashley a bit later and ask how Doc handled the rest of the day. He would not worry over a little misstep if that's all it had been.

"If I didn't know any better," Garrett said, interrupting Blake's thoughts. "I'd like to think you might like Ashley a bit more than what you're leading us to believe."

Garrett's statement had meant to be a joke, but it caught Blake off guard. Had his attraction to Ashley been that noticeable? He had no reason not to be attracted to her, but as far as acting on it, he wouldn't go there. He needed to focus on the ranch and keeping things in line. There was no way he could keep things straight if he was falling in love with his head in the clouds.

CHAPTER NINE

Ashley kept a close eye on her grandfather as they worked together through the morning hours. He'd guided Ashley through the process, taking her out to the main working area and showing her the process.

Gates clanked, followed by loud bellows throughout the morning as the ranch hands continued branding and leading the cattle through the chutes. With each new group, Ashley worked hard to get their ears tagged, matching the first year's calves with their cows and watching her grandfather administer their vaccines before turning them loose in the pasture. Ashley watched in awe at the process. From leading the herd in, to branding them with an electric branding tool, Ashley found no flaws in Blake's system.

"We're about done for the morning," her grandfather said, injecting a heifer with its required dose. "We'll head to the main house for lunch and enjoy some much-needed conversation while preparing for the second round."

Ashley went along with her grandfather's instructions as they finished out the last few heifers awaiting their tags and vaccinations. She was new to all of this —life on the ranch, practicing as a vet, and keeping pace with the rest of them. It was something she would have to get used to, and she would within time.

"How's Brycen adjusting to life on the ranch?"

Ashley set a new cartridge down on the table in front of her, ready to administer the next round. "I think he likes it here," she said, thinking about her son's excitement and the smile that hadn't left his face since arriving at the ranch.

"I had a feeling he would," her grandfather said with a slight grin. "A hard change from life in the city, but I think he's going to be just fine."

Ashley nodded. She thought about her own fears of adjusting to life on the ranch. She'd hesitated to make the move quite a few times in the last year until admitting it was necessary if she wanted to finish her schooling and become the veterinarian she'd always dreamed of becoming. Her grandfather had given her an opportunity she would have been silly not to take.

"How are you holding up?"

Her grandfather's question caught her off guard with the concern in his voice. She wasn't sure how to answer his question other than to say, "I'm hanging in there."

He offered a soft smile as he patted her on the arm. "You're going to do just fine here at the ranch. You just wait and see."

Ashley bundled the next set of tags together, waiting for the last few heifers to make their way through the chute and into their section. She'd caught an extra glance or two at her grandfather when he wasn't paying attention, looking for some kind of hint that things weren't what they seemed to be with him. He was getting older. There was no doubt about that. And if she were to be honest, she hated to think there was an underlying condition that had caused him to stumble and nearly fall while Blake had been standing next to him.

"Hey, Gramps," she said, thinking of the best approach in asking him a few questions about his health. He turned his attention away from the syringes and focused his eyes on her. She fought back the urge to leave well enough alone as she asked, "When was the last time a doctor saw you?"

His brows furrowed, and she knew it was a touchy subject. Her grandfather wasn't one to run to the doctor for every cough and sniffle. Not that she could blame him, because she couldn't remember the last time she'd seen her primary doctor, either. She'd made sure Brycen had his annual checkups and physicals for school, along with required vaccinations, but that was it.

She cleared her throat and approached the subject with a bit more understanding. "I don't like doctors that much either, but—"

"They quit handing out candy when we reached a certain age," her grandfather said with a laugh. She couldn't help but laugh along with him. He was good at cracking jokes and making light of heavy conversations, no matter how serious the situation. "No, that's not why I don't like going."

Ashley waited for him to say more, enlighten her about his thoughts and how he felt about being seen by an actual doctor. She understood being their own worst patients because she hardly batted an eye at self-treatment for her own symptoms. It had become easy to do when her husband needed her attention twenty-four seven, even with the hospice nurse's frequent visits near the end…

She shook her head, refocusing on what her grandfather was about to say. She had her own reasons for not seeing a doctor, and it had nothing to do with not wanting to stay healthy. It had everything to do with the possibility of receiving life-changing news. News that had the power to ricochet like misguided bullets, hitting innocent bystanders without hesitation. The power to flip someone's world upside down and inside out without giving them time to process what was happening, or what they were expected to do next.

"They always seem to have an opinion," her grandfather said, guiding Ashley back into the calving barn after releasing the last few heifers into the pasture. "And sometimes, I don't want to hear their opinions."

Her grandfather was feisty in his old age, not that she could blame him. It was the Irish and German in them that caused the stubbornness to shine through.

"I'm living my life the way I want to live it without having to hear their recommendations and cures for everything," he said. Without a pause, he continued, "There's a pill for everything nowadays, and who wants to take a handful of pills every day? Not me."

Ashley nodded along as her grandfather vented. She listened, wondering if there was a chance he knew something was wrong with his health, but he was ignoring it out of fear it could be something serious. Ashley wouldn't blame him if that were the case. She couldn't fathom hearing "you have cancer" or "I'm sorry there's no cure." Once had been enough, and she couldn't put into words what hearing those two sentences had caused the last time she'd heard them while holding her husband's hand and sobbing like a baby.

"You don't need to worry about me, Ash," he stated, offering her hand a gentle pat. "For as old as I am, I'm fine. I don't feel a year over ninety."

She cracked a smile at his last attempt at joking around. He was nowhere close to ninety. He still had a decade before he came close to his nineties.

"Alright," she said, squeezing his hand as she looked him in the eye. "But promise me you'll let me know when you don't feel like things are fine anymore?"

He offered her a subtle nod in agreement, but didn't make any promises. He stood from the wooden stool and held out his hand, offering her a hand up before leading her out of the calving barn and toward the main house.

Blake was standing near the front porch as they approached the house. Ashley had worked up an appetite and regretted not grabbing breakfast after sending Brycen off to school. "How are things going?"

"They're going as expected," her grandfather said before Ashley answered Blake's question. Instead, she went along with what he said by offering a reassuring smile. Blake wasn't asking about the cattle and working with tags and vaccines. He was asking about her grandfather—checking to make sure he hadn't had another spell.

"That's good to hear," Blake said, walking up the porch steps and into the house. He held the door for them before following them inside. "We have a couple more rounds of heifers to run through after lunch. It shouldn't take more than a few hours to get them done."

Her grandfather walked into the kitchen after hanging his hat on an empty hook and grabbed a plate of food. Mama Dixon greeted them as they followed his lead. She pulled Ashley to the side and offered her a plate of food that differed from the others. "I made your lunch extra special today," she said, handing the plate to Ashley. Ashley accepted it and thanked her, knowing better than to tell Mama Dixon she didn't have to. Mama Dixon enjoyed cooking for them, and it wasn't Ashley's place to tell her not to do something she wanted to, no matter how extra it seemed to be.

They moved through the line in rotation before making their way to the dining room and finding a spot to sit at the table. Much like at supper time, each person sat in the same spot, leaving an empty chair next to Blake. Ashley didn't argue when Blake pulled out the chair for her this time. Instead, she sat down and thanked him for being the gentleman that he was.

"How good are you at numbers?"

Blake's question was out of the blue, and it took Ashley a minute to realize he was talking to her. She looked around the table, realizing everyone was minding their own while devouring the lunch Mama Dixon had provided for them.

She took a bite and shrugged. "I can't say that math was my favorite in school."

Blake grunted as he took a bite of food. "Can't say that it was mine, either."

Ashley wondered what prompted him to ask such a question. She wondered if it had anything to do with vaccinating the cattle with the appropriate dose, or if he was just making light conversation to pass the time.

"I remember the boys bringing home their report cards from school," Mama Dixon chimed in from the other end of the table. "He's not lying about math being his least favorite subject in school."

Blake tossed his mother a quick glance before laughing it off. Ashley couldn't remember the last time she received anything less than a B+ in math. High school algebra had never been a challenge for her.

Ashley studied Blake for a minute, waiting for him to give a reason for such a random question, but when he said nothing further, she shrugged it off and focused on eating her lunch.

"We're going to need extra watch on the pastures

at night," Blake announced once the last few ranch hands were settled at the table. "Garrett and I have noticed the cattle are looking quite rough and seem to have a hard time settling. If there are predators running the fence line at all hours of the night, it's causing a disturbance that I'd like to take care of before it's too late."

Ashley sat back in her chair, listening and wondering what predators were lurking in the woods near the ranch. Montana was well known for mountain lions and wolves, and she wouldn't doubt they were on the move while looking for their next meal.

"What can I do to help?" Ashley asked. If she could do something to help ease Blake's worry and protect the livestock, she would in a heartbeat.

Snickers from the younger ranch hands crowded the far end of the table, and Blake shot them a stern look that told them to knock it off. She couldn't help but notice his dark brown eyes and the sharp edge of his jawline as she sat next to him.

She averted her eyes, not wanting to get caught admiring how handsome the man sitting next to her was. The last thing she needed was to find herself attracted to Blake. He was her complete opposite, not to mention the boss of the ranch. She couldn't afford to fall head over heels for a guy who could turn around and put an end to finishing her dreams.

"Aside from hourly checks on birthing cows, I

need eyes on the perimeter of the property line," Blake said, ignoring Ashley's question all together. If he didn't want her help, why wouldn't he just say it? "Garrett and I noticed a lot this morning while rounding up the cattle. With them losing weight, come spring, we won't see a profitable return on them in the market. We need to work together to provide extra feed while keeping a close eye on what's lurking."

Ashley watched several ranch hands nod their heads in agreement without missing a beat. Blake had a solid crew on board with protecting the livestock, but Ashley still felt like there was something she could do to help as well.

"What can I do?" she asked again, this time much quieter, so only Blake could hear her. She didn't want to draw attention to the fact she was desperate for an answer.

Blake finished his lunch and took a quick drink from his glass before giving her an answer. His eyes focused on her, causing a sudden jolt to cascade through her body, starting with her heart. A breath caught in her throat as she waited for him to say something, anything.

"I just need you to be on standby in case there's an attack on the livestock," Blake said, looking to the others for understanding. "I need everyone to keep a close watch on the livestock and be ready for anything. Garrett and I will keep a close eye on the fence line tonight and make sure there aren't any breaks. But starting tomorrow, we're going to need all hands on deck."

Ashley nodded as her grandfather patted her leg. She turned to face him. He gave her a concerned look before saying, "I want you to be careful. You have a lot more to protect than those cattle. I don't want you out wandering the property after dark."

Blake cleared his throat and leaned forward, resting his arms on the table. "Don't worry, Doc. I'll keep a close eye on her and Brycen."

Ashley turned back to face Blake. "You don't have to do that. I'm capable of handling things on my own," she said, realizing Blake wasn't having any of that. "I mean, it's not like we're going to be roaming the property at midnight. We'll be in our nice, warm beds."

There was something Blake wasn't telling her, or maybe she'd said something wrong. She just couldn't sit back and act like she wasn't capable of helping on the ranch with whatever needed done.

"If it's what I think it is," Blake started, "it won't matter if it's day or night. Be aware of your surroundings at all times. And that includes the kids, too."

Blake's eyes found hers before he looked around the table, making sure everyone was on the same page. Ashley thought about Brycen and Allie racing around the property, having fun like kids were supposed to. How was she supposed to tell Brycen he needed to stay close to the house and not wander too far out of sight? And what did Blake think was creeping around the land?

CHAPTER TEN

Blake hadn't meant to put the fear of God in Ashley, but he wanted to make sure everyone sitting at the table knew how dangerous it could get once the pack of wolves moved closer to the ranch.

He needed her to know, and Becca as well, that the kids would need to stay close. Winter months were a challenge on the ranch in more ways than Blake cared to think about. From keeping the weight on the livestock, to keeping things running, and keeping hungry predators off the ranch.

"Let's get things finished for the day," he announced, causing his brothers and the ranch hands to break into formation. With the way things went that morning, Blake figured they'd call it a night by suppertime.

"Hey, Blake. Got a minute?"

Blake stopped and turned to face Ashley, who was walking down the porch steps and heading right for him. She shielded her eyes from the mid-day sun as she approached him.

"What's up?" he asked, ignoring the subtle scent of lavender and honey as she stepped in front of him.

"I'm willing to help in any way that I can," Ashley said. Her eyes locked on his, and for a minute he couldn't think of what to say. Since when had he paid attention to her eyes or the way her hair fell over her shoulders in waves over her winter coat? "I meant what I said."

He cleared his throat, clearing the distracting thoughts from his mind. "And I meant what I said, too. Have you ever seen a pack of wolves on the hunt?"

She shook her head, a concerned look filled her eyes. She didn't know a thing about living in the mountains. He wouldn't expect a city girl to know how dangerous things could get.

"I just need you to promise me you'll keep a close eye on Brycen and be aware of your surroundings at all times," Blake said. He needed her to understand that their safety was his top priority when it came down to it. The last thing he wanted was for Ashley or Brycen to get hurt because he hadn't made it clear to her. "I've got my brothers and the ranch hands to look after the livestock. That's our job. Your job is to protect your son and be ready to help Doc if there's an attack on the herd."

"Of course," she said, the look of concern long gone as she accepted her role on the ranch. He couldn't take the chance of anyone getting hurt—especially Ashley and Brycen.

"Okay," he said, placing his cowboy hat on top of his head. "Let's get back to work."

He turned and expected her to walk off after Doc, but she paused and asked, "Why'd you ask if I was good at math?"

Turning back to face her, he hesitated a minute before saying, "I've got some problems with things not adding up in the books. No matter how many times I've studied the books, I can't seem to find where I went wrong."

Ashley offered a gentle smile. Her lips were a soft shade of pink, and he found himself distracted by thoughts of kissing her. He shook his head, pulling himself away from those distracting thoughts. "Nevermind I mentioned it. I'm sure I'll figure it out. I'll take another look at the books tonight after supper."

He kicked himself for allowing his thoughts to focus on Ashley like that. Since when did he ever let a woman distract him from getting his work done? They'd already lost ten minutes just standing there.

Blake turned once again, prepared to get back to work, but Ashley stopped him before he got too far.

"I can take a look if you'd like," she said, giving a quick shrug and an offer Blake couldn't turn down. "I'll bring Brycen along, and he can do his homework while I look at what you've got."

"Sure," he said, struggling to accept her offer while knowing it wouldn't be good to get too close to her. "We'll figure out something after supper, then."

Ashley nodded and walked off toward the gates. He watched her walk away, wondering what kind of mess he'd gotten himself into.

"I DON'T LIKE THE LOOK OF THIS," ASHLEY SAID, pointing to the dark red number occupying a space on the spreadsheet. Brycen was in the next room, working on his homework, while Blake had Ashley sitting at his desk in the main office. They'd agreed to meet right after supper, and Ashley wasted no time getting to work on the books. "It looks like something is off with the payments, but I won't know for sure unless you have invoices from last year."

Blake stood from the spot next to Ashley and walked over to a nearby file cabinet. "Curt kept everything filed in here," he said, sliding open the drawer and looking at the individual tabs on each folder. "I've got the last two years in these middle drawers, and the current year in this top one."

"Let's start from the bottom and work our way to the top," Ashley said, her suggestion making sense to Blake as he dug through the folders and pulled out January from two years back. January seemed like a good place to start. "Thanks," she said as he placed the folder in front of her.

Blake watched as she thumbed through the folder, looking at past receipts and invoices he had no clue about. He'd thought about calling on Curt, bringing him into the office to work through the dilemma, but held off until he hit a dead end. If Ashley couldn't figure it out, Blake would have no choice but to bring Curt in.

"Hmm," Ashley said, looking over the last of the invoices and matching them to the spreadsheet. "January looks good. I'm not finding any discrepancies here."

Blake nodded, pushing himself out of the chair next to her and walking over to the file cabinet. He placed a red *X* on the tab next to January before placing the folder back in the drawer. He pulled out February's folder and handed it to Ashley as he sat down next to her. The process seemed never ending and redundant since he'd already checked over the files. It didn't hurt to have Ashley looking them over for a second time in case he had missed something.

And he wouldn't deny the fact it seemed less of a thorn in his side with her sitting next to him.

"When did Curt quit the books and hire someone else to look after them?" Ashley asked, thumbing through the papers and studying the numbers.

"I'm not a hundred percent sure about that," Blake said, knowing his uncle had kept the books under wraps and hardly talked about finances with the Dixon brothers. "I'd like to think it was some time over the last year he managed the ranch before deciding to move back to Maple Glen."

Ashley glanced over her shoulder at him. Her blue eyes focused on him for a minute before asking, "Didn't someone say he was living next door at the old Riggs' farm? When did he move back to Woodford Creek?"

Blake laughed it off and said, "Yeah, he moved in next door a couple of months ago, once Shyann put it up for sale."

"Shyann? Like, Garrett's Shyann?" Ashley's brow furrowed in concentration as she tried to put the pieces together. There were a lot of things that happened throughout the past year as the Dixon brothers settled into the ownership of the ranch. His brothers finding love had been just the start of it.

"Yes, that Shyann," Blake confirmed, remembering when she'd come back after her father's funeral. "She'd been on the fence about keeping or selling the house she'd grown up in, but once she and Garrett worked together, it was a done deal as they gave love a second chance."

Love was something Blake had a hard time finding, though he'd come close a time or two.

"That's really sweet," Ashley said, turning her attention back to the books. "Second chances are always something you see in the movies, but never in real life."

Blake wanted to know more about Ashley and how she'd found her way to the ranch. Of course, part of it had to deal with Doc bringing her on board, but what had happened in her life to make Doc offer her such an opportunity?

"I've seen it happen a time or two," Blake said, thinking about Uncle Curt and Aunt Fran as well as his brother, Garrett, and Shyann. "Love has a way of finding us when we least expect it, I guess. Even though I haven't had much luck with that. The only thing that ever finds me is trouble."

Sharing a quick laugh, Ashley shook her head. "For some reason, I'm not having any trouble believing that."

"Hey, now," he said with a laugh as he leaned back in his chair. "I consider myself quite lucky. I don't have to worry about some woman taking my heart and shattering it into a million pieces. Plus, it gives me more time to focus on the ranch without worrying about distractions."

He caught Ashley's eyes for a split second before she diverted her attention back to the spreadsheet in front of her. There was something in the way she'd looked at him. She'd opened her mouth to say something, but bit her lip and refocused on the task in front of her.

"Can I ask you something without you getting mad?"

She looked up from the papers in front of her. "Why would I get mad?"

He offered a slight shrug and said, "I just don't want to upset you."

Ashley leaned back away from the desk as she repositioned herself in the chair in order to face him. "There aren't many things that upset me. You can ask me anything," she said, a look of uncertainty crossing her face. "I'd like to think I'm an open book, even though I'm always careful not to share too much…"

Her words trailed off, causing him to rethink his question. He wanted to know her better. For whatever reason, he'd never cared to know someone like he cared to know her.

"What's your story?"

She kicked back with a soft laugh. "My story?"

"Yeah, your story," Blake said. "Doc didn't say much about where you and Brycen were moving here from or what caused you to put off getting your degree in veterinary medicine..."

He allowed his words to trail off as he watched her expression change to one of uncertainty and doubt. He didn't want to push her into giving him information. If she wasn't willing to talk about her life before the ranch, it was more than okay with him.

Ashley leaned forward, resting her elbows against her knees. She opened her mouth, ready to say something, when Brycen walked up behind her into the small office. Blake watched as she clammed up and turned her attention to her son.

"Hey, buddy, what's up?"

Brycen walked over to the desk and leaned against it. He studied the papers scattered across the desk and said, "Just seeing what you are doing."

Ashley reached out for her son's arm and brought him in for a side hug. "Blake and I are working on a few things. Is your homework done for tomorrow?"

Brycen gave an over exaggerated nod. "Can I go see if Allie wants to go swing on the tire?"

Ashley gave the young boy permission, but told him to check in with her in a few minutes. "Don't wander too far, okay? I want to make sure I can still see you from here."

Blake thought about what he'd told Ashley about the wolves. He hadn't wanted her to tell Brycen about them to scare him, and he trusted her to keep her son safe.

"Hey, Brycen," Blake called out, catching the young boy before he ran out the door. Brycen turned around and came back into the office. As he stood in front of Blake, looking him in the eye with the same soft blue eyes he shared with his mother, Blake said, "Remember what I said about keeping your distance from the animals?"

"Yes, sir," Brycen said with a firm nod. "I can only go around them when I have an adult with me."

Blake smiled and patted the kid on the back. "Good deal. Maybe when you and Allie get off the bus tomorrow, I can show you the new calves?"

Brycen's face lit up with a smile. "That would be awesome!"

Excitement radiated in waves from the boy, and Blake couldn't imagine what it would be like for a ten-year-old to see livestock up close and personal for the first time.

"Alright, then that's what we'll do," Blake said, glancing over at Ashley, who was watching the interaction with a soft smile on her face. "As long as your mom says it's okay," he added.

Brycen turned toward her. She was already going along with the plan without Brycen having to ask for permission. Blake looked at her then, a smile pulling at his lips as he thought about making an evening out of it before supper. "Maybe she can come along too, if she wants."

Without hesitation, Ashley said, "I would like that, but first, I need to figure out the mess we have going on here."

Brycen told his mother he loved her and that he would be back to check in. It didn't take long for the front door to slam behind him before Brycen was long gone and headed toward Drew and Becca's cabin.

Blake watched him through the office window, wanting to make sure he got where he was going. It didn't take long for Allie to rush out of the cabin and race him to the old tree with the tire swing. He made it a point to help keep an eye on him while Ashley opened up about their life back in the city.

He leaned forward, getting comfortable sitting next to her, and waited for her to tell her story as he got the feeling Ashley was holding something back.

CHAPTER ELEVEN

Ashley flipped through the papers in front of her, willing herself to open up to Blake. He didn't need to know everything, but knowing the gist of it would assure him she wasn't a threat to the ranch. Although, he should have realized that by now. She was more than willing to help him and the ranch any way she could, even if that meant staying up late at night and keeping an eye on the livestock.

Blake shifted in his chair, leaning forward as he waited for her to say something. She wasn't sure where to start. She looked out the window, checking on Brycen and Allie. They were swinging each other on the tire under the tree. It was good to see her son happy.

"What made you step back from finishing your degree?"

Blake's question pulled her attention away from her son and his new friend. She shifted in her chair, leaning back and getting comfortable before saying, "I didn't have much choice." Her answer didn't seem to appease Blake, so she added, "My husband was diagnosed with stage four cancer soon after I started the program."

Blake stayed quiet next to her, leaning back in his chair with a sympathetic look on his face. Ashley looked down at the papers in front of her, debating on whether to look through them while talking about her painful past. Maybe if she had something to focus on, talking about it wouldn't be too difficult.

"I couldn't go to school, take care of Brycen, and look after Colin…" She allowed her words to trail off, recalling the toughest time in her life. She had tried so hard to be the best at everything, making sure her son and husband were taken care of, but she'd failed. "I couldn't juggle everything at the same time. I had to let go of something, and it sure wasn't going to be my husband or our child."

Blake leaned forward, reaching out a hand and placing it on top of Ashley's. Giving it a gentle squeeze, he said, "I'm sorry, Ash. I had no idea."

"Not too many people know." She had kept to herself through a time when she needed someone the most. Old friendships had fizzled out soon after the diagnosis, which left her with no one to talk to. "Brycen was seven when Colin was first diagnosed. Colin lost his battle soon after Brycen turned eight."

It had been a hard six months. It had been even more difficult to celebrate a birthday, knowing the father of her child wouldn't make it to the next one. Ashley pulled it off the best she knew how at the time while knowing she didn't have a choice in the matter.

"That's..." Blake's sentence trailed off as she looked at him. The look in his eyes told Ashley that he understood the pain she'd felt. "I lost my dad at a young age, too."

Ashley glanced out the window, checking on her son and Allie. Both were still hanging out by the tire swing, chasing each other around the base, laughing and carrying on. "I can't imagine what it's like to lose someone at that age," she stated. She'd lost both of her parents shortly after her wedding—the second and third deaths Brycen had to cope with. It had been hard enough for Ashley to cope with the losses, and adding her son's struggles right along with hers... she still wasn't sure how she hadn't broken into a million splintered pieces.

"It's difficult for sure," Blake said. Ashley realized he hadn't moved his hand from hers since he first placed it on top of hers. "I was six, and my brothers were about two and four. Our father was a proud bull rider and nothing would hold him back. He entered a rodeo about fifteen hundred miles from home in Texas."

Blake's pause caused Ashley to stop what she was doing and focus on him. She'd thumbed through the papers to focus on something other than her emotions. Distract herself from crying ugly tears in front of Blake. That seemed to fail now, though, as Blake shared the pain she'd imagined her son had felt at the time of losing his own father—continued to feel while living life without the one every young boy looked up to.

"I still remember Ma getting the call, but I don't remember much else other than Ma's uncontrollable sobbing as she hung up the phone in the kitchen, and then seeing my father in the casket…"

Blake's words trailed off, and Ashley held back the emotion threatening to escape. She wanted to say something to acknowledge Blake's pain, but the only thing she could manage was a gentle squeeze of his hand as she said, "I'm sorry."

The office door burst open, and the two young kids ran inside, interrupting a vulnerable time between her and Blake. She wiped away the stray tears that had fallen regardless of her failed attempt at keeping her emotions in check.

"Something's wrong," Brycen stated, a panicked expression on his face. Allie, too, as she stood beside

Brycen, trying her best to get Blake's attention. "In the pasture."

Adrenaline rushed through Ashley as she stood from the chair and let go of Blake's hand. Blake was on his feet next to her in a matter of seconds as they tried their best to get the fear-ridden kids to explain what they'd seen or heard.

"The cows," Brycen said, struggling to get his words out between the panicked breaths. "They're making horrible sounds, and I think I heard howling."

Blake hurried to a nearby cabinet, reaching in for a shotgun before turning and heading out the door. Ashley raced out the door behind him, telling the kids to stay inside while praying the herd of cattle in the pasture was okay.

Blake carried the shotgun in one hand while radioing for the ranch hands to meet him in the north pasture. Ashley raced to keep up with him as she prayed Brycen and Allie would follow her instruction to stay inside.

Four wheelers came from all directions on the ranch, aiding Blake in his search of what was happening in the middle of the pasture. Ashley couldn't tell what was happening with the herd until she approached the gate.

Her mouth fell open as she witnessed a pack of wolves in a standoff with the herd while surrounding a cow and its calf. Blake fired a warning shot in the air, but the pack kept their stance as they threatened to attack again.

The ranch hands raced through the open gate on their four wheelers as Ashley followed them on foot out to the middle of the pasture. Blake fired another shot, aiming straight for the leader of the pack. The wolf dropped to the ground, guarding his back leg.

"Blake, stop," Ashley called out, not sure why she cared to protect the wild predators who were wreaking havoc on the herd. Blake shot a look at her as he kept his distance from the pack. The ranch hands fired several shots, a failed attempt to scare off the rest. "What do we do?"

The adrenaline rushed through Ashley as she realized the wolves weren't backing away from the injured cow. The calf stayed close to its mother's side while Ashley fought back the urge to rush in and pick it up. She didn't want the wolves to pounce on the newborn calf.

"Ashley, don't!" Blake shouted above the chaos. Cattle bellowed in a standoff with the wolves—unphased by the shotgun blasts surrounding them. "Ashley!"

Ashley was too close to the calf and its mama now. She couldn't turn back. She needed to save the baby before it was too late.

As she approached the calf and the injured cow, she realized it was already too late to save the mama.

The wolves had attacked her, leaving her no choice but to succumb to the injuries she sustained during her attempt at keeping her baby safe.

Ashley held back her emotions as she lifted the calf in her arms and carried it out of harm's way. She ignored the angry look on Blake's face as she carried the calf past him and the ranch hands. She was on a mission to save the calf and refused to stop now.

One last gunshot echoed throughout the property as the wolves admitted defeat and took off in the opposite direction. She watched as the injured wolf hobbled after the rest of the pack. Ashley focused on the calf in her arms, avoiding what was happening behind her.

"Mom!" Brycen called out from the other side of the fence, and her stomach dropped. She had given him specific orders to stay inside. "Is it okay?"

A look of panic crossed Brycen's face as he met Ashley on the other side of the gate. "I thought I told you to stay inside."

She couldn't help but scold him for not listening, even though she had failed to listen when Blake had told her to stop as well. Brycen's brows furrowed with an angry expression on his face. "I'm sorry, Mom. I wanted to make sure you were okay."

Ashley's heart melted as she set the unscathed newborn calf down and closed the gate behind her.

She wanted to scold Brycen for not listening, but she couldn't blame him for not staying inside.

Tears streamed down his face, and he fought to wipe them away, leaving dirt marks across his cheeks. She reached out to him as she knelt down in front of him. "Come here, Bry."

Ashley wrapped her arms around her son's middle and pulled him in close to her. She placed a hand on the back of his head, encouraging him to rest against her shoulder. "It's okay. We're okay."

Her son cried on her shoulder, releasing the emotions he'd held back for what must have seemed like forever for a ten-year-old. She should have never left the two kids in the office alone. She hadn't been thinking after seeing Blake grab his gun.

"I'm sorry," he whispered as he snuggled into her. She held him close and told him everything would be okay.

Blake walked up to the gate behind them, and she prayed he would keep his anger under control. It had been a scary situation for everyone, and she already regretted leaving her son and Allie behind.

Ashley moved Brycen and the calf off to the side and out of the way as she looked up at Blake.

"Is the calf injured?" he asked, holding the gate open for the ranch hands so they could pass through on the four wheelers. If he was angry with her foolishness, he was doing a good job of hiding it in front of Brycen.

"Not that I can tell, but I haven't had a chance to look her over."

Brycen let go of Ashley as he looked down at the calf. "Is her mom okay?"

Ashley glanced up at Blake and shook her head. Blake combed a hand through his hair as she explained what happened to the calf's mother.

"What are we going to do now?" Brycen's voice quivered as he looked down at the calf, then back at Ashley and Blake. "She needs her mom, doesn't she?"

"She'll be okay without her mom, bud," Blake said, setting the gun down as he knelt in front of Brycen. "We'll keep her extra warm in the barn and give her plenty of milk to drink. Do you want to help us do that?"

With tear-filled eyes, Brycen nodded his head. "What about Allie? Can she help, too?"

Ashley looked toward the office building, relieved to see Becca and Allie walking toward them. Thankfully, Allie hadn't chased after Brycen. Ashley wasn't sure what Allie's response would have been to seeing the chaos unfold.

"Of course," Blake said. "The more the merrier."

"Is everything okay? Allie came to get me, even though I was halfway out the door when I heard the commotion." Becca and Allie approached Brycen's side as Ashley looked over the calf.

"It will be," Blake said. He was standing behind Ashley and waiting for his brothers to meet him at the gate.

Becca nodded as she wrapped an arm around Allie and held her close to her side. "I think we're going to head inside, but let me know if there's anything I can do."

Both Blake and Ashley accepted her offer and watched the two of them walk back to their cabin.

Ashley was coming down from the rush of adrenaline as she looked up at Blake. Everything happened so fast, she had no choice but to take action. "Should I call Gramps to come and take a look at the calf?"

She was admitting her lack of knowledge with livestock, but she would not let that stand in the way of helping a newborn calf survive without its mother.

Blake knelt down beside her and checked over the calf. "Why don't you and Brycen take the calf to the homestead and grab some blankets from the closet," Blake suggested. "We can have Doc look over the calf in the morning while he's here finishing up with the annual tests."

Ashley agreed, knowing her grandfather wasn't a full-time veterinarian for the ranch. He was a community vet, hired on by several small-town ranchers to look after and care for their livestock. It was his way of making a living. He'd explained it to her prior to coming to Montana. He'd mentioned having to bounce from ranch to ranch, but he would let her stick around the Dixon Ranch until she was comfortable visiting other ranches with him.

"I'm going to round up my brothers and check on the fence line. There's no telling how that pack got into our pasture, but I want to make sure it doesn't happen again."

Ashley lifted the calf into her arms. This time, she felt the weight of the calf without the aid of adrenaline. She looked down at Brycen as they headed for the main house and asked him to get the door for her.

She wasn't sure what Mama Dixon would say about having a newborn calf in the house, but Ashley followed Blake's orders anyway.

She carried the calf through the house and into the back laundry room. There, she asked Brycen to grab the towels hanging nearby. They needed to dry the calf off in order to warm her up. Fresh snow had fallen throughout the evening, and there was no way to tell when it had been born.

"I'll go look for blankets, Mom," Brycen said. She was proud of him for taking it upon himself to help. "I'll be right back."

Ashley stayed by the calf's side, trying her best to keep her emotions in check while keeping the poor thing warm. She understood it was only part of nature that wolves would prey on the vulnerable, but she didn't have to like it.

"Well, look what we have here," Mama Dixon said as she walked into the back room. "Hey, there, Sweet Pea."

Ashley looked up from her spot on the floor, holding the calf in her lap with a hopeful heart that it would survive without its mama.

CHAPTER TWELVE

Blake climbed on a four wheeler and rode alongside his brother looking for a hole in the fence line. His thoughts carried him back to the chaos, wrapping Ashley into the center of it all. He hadn't felt a greater need to protect someone than he felt tonight when she took it upon herself to rescue the calf.

What would he have done if Ashley had gotten hurt? He didn't like to think about what could have happened when she walked straight into the ring of fire without hesitation. She was an animal lover, there was no doubt about that, but where did she draw the line when it came to her own safety?

"Still coming down from the adrenaline rush?"

Garrett's question pulled Blake from his thoughts as he came to a stop near a gaping hole in the fence.

What they'd gone through tonight had spiked his adrenaline, but he wouldn't admit the real reason he was quiet.

"Looks like another one of Big Red's doings," Garrett announced as he climbed off his four wheeler. "I don't think there's a way to keep that heifer from breaking out."

They had just checked the fence prior to heading in for supper. Blake hadn't thought the darn heifer would make an escape through the enforced fencing Garrett and Mason replaced from Curt's property.

"Remember when I mentioned that Big Red escaping was going to cost us?"

Blake hated that his brother was right. It wasn't like Blake hadn't listened, though. That darn heifer had a mind of her own and would continue to find a way out, no matter how many times they repaired or replaced the fence.

"This time she cost one of her own," Garrett said as he inspected the break in the fence. "How in the world did she break through that?"

Blake shrugged. He didn't have the answer to that question. He wasn't sure how Big Red escaped every time they'd least expected it. "We can't keep the predators out if she keeps letting them in."

"You're right about that," Garrett said. He climbed on the four wheeler and turned back toward the main property. "I'll round up some ranch hands to come out and help me patch it up. I'll be sure to bring plenty of ammunition back with us."

The night was still young, but dark was setting in. A seasonal change Blake could never get used to as they approached the winter months. He didn't care for the sun to set so soon after supper, cutting several of his working hours when he was used to working until eight at night.

He looked around, listening for any sign of the pack's return. They would have to take care of the cow in the middle of the pasture before calling it a night, or the pack would be back in search of it.

Once Blake cleaned up, he headed to the main house in search of Ashley and Brycen. He'd sent them inside long before calling it a night, and if he were to be honest, he wanted to check in and see how they were doing—especially Brycen. He'd taken a liking to the kid soon after meeting him, and he couldn't help but feel an immediate connection after learning about the death of his father.

Blake had been six when his father passed away, and he knew how hard it had been to cope with that loss. His father's loss still bothered him to this day, causing him to think about how things could have been different if his father hadn't chased the thrill of bronc and bull riding. If his father had stayed home, sat that one rodeo out, and enjoyed spending time with his family…

Blake shook the thoughts away as he climbed the porch steps and walked inside. It was late, an illumination from the back room being the only light in the house. He let the light guide him to the back room as he anticipated seeing who he'd find on the other side of the door.

As he pushed open the door, he found Brycen curled up next to his mother, cocooned in a blanket by her side as she cradled both the young boy and the motherless calf. He watched as she stroked her fingers over the calf's face, relaxing and coaxing it to sleep.

She looked up, meeting his eyes with hers, and he couldn't ignore the way she made him question everything he once believed about love.

"I'd ask how it's going in here, but from the looks of it, you have everything under control," Blake said. He slid a hamper out of his way as he prepared an empty spot next to Ashley. He sat down beside her, careful not to disturb the sleeping boy or the calf.

"She already has a name," Ashley whispered. Blake wanted to tell her they rarely named them, but the look in her eyes caught him off guard. If they wanted to name the calf, then so be it.

"And what name is that?"

"Sweet Pea." Ashley smiled and offered a cute shrug. "That's what Mama Dixon calls her."

"Sounds about right." Blake grinned as he reached out to pet the calf. "What'd Ma think about her?"

Ashley's smile faded as she stroked the calf's side. "She's not too happy it lost its mama, but she's thankful we were there to save it."

Blake thought about it for a minute before saying, "You know you could have been seriously injured, Ash."

She gave a subtle shrug and carried on with soothing the calf in her lap. He didn't want to get upset with her, but he wanted her to realize just how much danger she'd put herself in when she went for the calf.

"Those wolves weren't backing down," Blake stated, recalling the adrenaline that coursed through him as he had watched Ashley run into the middle of it all. The need to protect her had been stronger than anything he'd ever felt. "They could've turned on you before giving me a chance to protect you."

She looked up then, her warm blue eyes stirred with emotion as she focused on him. "I did what any mother would do for a baby, Blake. I couldn't just stand by and let her get hurt."

Blake sat there, speechless. How was he supposed to tell a mother that she'd done the wrong thing? It was a mother's instinct to protect and save the young, he knew that, but he also knew that, given the situation, Ashley should have stayed back and waited for a better time to grab the calf.

Blake shifted, getting comfortable on the tiled laundry room floor. He had taken some time thinking about how he'd reacted when he first learned about her moving into the spare cabin. He had regrets for acting like a jerk instead of being grateful Doc had an extra set of hands to help him while working with the cattle.

"Ash, I want you to know something," Blake said. She looked up at him with those soft blue eyes of hers, and he fought against the urge to kiss her. He wasn't looking to fall in love with her. Her stay on the ranch was temporary. She was only there to finish out her internship before moving on with her life and taking Brycen with her. "I just want you to know that I'm happy you're here. Doc's not getting any younger, and I know this ranch isn't his only concern."

A concerned expression crossed Ashley's face, willing Blake to get to the point. "I just want you to know that you're more than welcome to stay on the ranch for however long you'd like… or need to."

She nodded, accepting his offer.

"I know the books tell a different story, but I'd like to hire you on as a part-time bookkeeper," Blake said, realizing right now might not be the best time to offer her a second job on the ranch. He needed to figure out the money situation before getting himself in too deep, but he couldn't help wanting to keep Ashley on the ranch. He cared about her and Brycen. "I'll split my pay with you just to make it work. I've got too many things I need to focus on around here to worry about the books from month to month."

Ashley smiled with a nod before saying, "I think I'd like that. I was going to talk to Gramps about this whole vet thing, anyway."

Blake straightened as he studied her. "What about this whole vet thing?"

Ashley shook her head as she continued stroking the calf's side. She kept her voice to a whisper as she explained, "I'm just not sure I'm cut out for this kind of stuff."

Blake tried to interrupt. He attempted to tell her she was good at being Doc's right hand, but she wasn't having it. She shook her head again and said, "I've been thinking a lot about it lately, and I can't pretend like I know what I'm doing when I don't have a clue about livestock."

Was she thinking about backing out of the veterinarian program? Blake couldn't wrap his head around the reason she would do such a thing.

"Isn't being a veterinarian something you've wanted for a long time?" Blake questioned, waiting for her to tell him what had caused her to change her mind. "I mean, I've seen the way you handle the cattle. You tagged them like a pro, and I'm sure Doc would say the same."

An unsettling emotion crossed her face as Blake turned toward her. "Ash, what's going on? What's making you change your mind?"

Ashley released a heavy sigh as she leaned her head back against the washing machine. "I've been thinking about it for a while now," she admitted, closing her eyes. "But after tonight… seeing that cow lying helpless in the pasture after being attacked…"

"We were too late," Blake stated, trying his best to comfort her. "That wasn't your fault. There was nothing either of us could have done to save her."

Ashley's eyes filled with tears as she looked at him. He reached out and took hold of her hand, comforting her the best way he knew how. "Ash, I know it was hard to see. It's not something I'm happy about either, but sometimes that's just a part of life on the ranch. Things happen that are out of our control, and there's nothing we can do about it."

He reached up and ran his thumb against her cheek, drying the tears as they streamed down her face. His heart ached to comfort her, to reassure her they'd done everything they could have done to save the mama. He'd known they were out there, scouting the fence line and planning their attack. He and his ranch hands had done their best to protect the herd, but Blake knew deep down that no matter how hard they tried, the attack was inevitable.

"It has nothing to do with your ability as a vet," Blake stated matter-of-factly, keeping his voice low. "You can't back out of doing something you've wanted to do your whole life just because one thing didn't go as planned."

"If I couldn't save her, how am I supposed to believe that I have what it takes to save the others?" Ashley spoke softly as she questioned Blake. He didn't have the answers she was looking for. All he knew was there was no way he was going to let her give up on her dreams.

He traced his thumb along her jawline, thinking of a way to convince her to hold on to her dreams for a little while longer. "It's not your job to save them all, Ash. Even Doc will tell you that. There have been plenty of cattle Doc couldn't save, and there's no doubt in my mind that there will be plenty more. It's just how things are when you work on a ranch. It's something you have to get used to."

Blake had a hard time with a few of the losses he'd witnessed while growing up on the ranch. He'd learned the hard way not to get too attached to the cattle because there were too many things that made them vulnerable—the heat, parasites, predators. The only thing they could do was to try their best to prevent those things from happening.

Ashley relaxed against the washing machine as she laid her head back and closed her eyes. She was having a hard time dealing with the loss she'd witnessed tonight, but Blake would be the one to see her through it. He didn't want her to give up. There was no doubt in his mind that she would be a great asset on the ranch. Whether it be working alongside Doc with the livestock, or working through the books. Either way, Blake wasn't giving up on her, and he certainly didn't want to see her give up on herself.

"It's getting late," she whispered as she looked down at the sleeping child next to her. Brycen had slept without stirring while curled up next to his mother. "I should get Brycen home and tucked into bed."

Blake nodded as he stood to his feet. He carefully picked up the calf as he waited for Ashley to get to her feet. He watched as she gently shifted her leg out from underneath Brycen before standing up. Blake held a hand to steady her as she maneuvered around the crowded room.

He carefully set the calf down on the bed of blankets before turning his attention to Brycen. He looked back at Ashley and asked, "Would you like me to carry him home?"

Without hesitation, she accepted his offer before he squatted down to lift Brycen into his arms. The ten-year-old wasn't as heavy as Blake expected, so carrying him home wasn't all that hard to accomplish. The trick was to keep him close and resting against Blake's shoulder without waking him up.

Ashley wrapped the blanket around Brycen before stepping out of the laundry room. Blake followed her to the front door and smiled when she held it open for them.

The warmth of the child warmed Blake's heart as he carried him from the main house to Ashley's cabin. It was a short distance between the two, and by the time they arrived at Ashley's, Blake wished it had taken longer as he approached the bottom of the porch steps.

"Want me to carry him inside for you?" Blake asked as he climbed the front steps. Ashley gave a quick nod before opening the door and following them inside. She pointed to the loft upstairs and followed Blake up to Brycen's room.

Once Brycen was in bed and tucked in for the night, Blake walked back downstairs and out to the porch. He turned to face Ashley as she walked out behind him.

"Thank you," she whispered into the darkness surrounding them. Blake took a step, closing the distance between them before taking a hold of her hand. "You have nothing to thank me for. I only did what any gentleman would have done."

Ashley smiled into the darkness, the warmth of

her breath warm against his face as he stared into her eyes. The smell of lavender and honey lingered between them. "Goodnight, Blake."

"Goodnight, Ash," he said, ignoring the urge to kiss her as he turned and headed down the steps. He watched as she walked inside, offering one last wave before closing the door.

CHAPTER THIRTEEN

"Is Sweet Pea going to be okay, Mom?"

Brycen sat at the kitchen table while Ashley cooked breakfast for the two of them. She'd spent most of the night thinking about the calf and the trauma it had gone through less than twelve hours ago.

"I'm sure she'll be just fine," Ashley said as she flipped a pancake on the griddle. "I'll have Gramps look at her this morning after I see you off to school."

Her son groaned and grumbled as he colored a dinosaur picture at the table. "I wish I didn't have to go to school."

Ashley stacked the pancakes onto a plate and carried it to the table, along with syrup and butter. "I thought you liked school."

Brycen shrugged. "It's okay, I guess. But I'd rather be here with you."

Ashley's heart melted at her son's confession. He was at the age where he was practicing his independence, so it was nice to know he still wanted to spend time with her.

"Well, I'll still be here when you get home." She set the plate of pancakes in the center of the table and sat down next to Brycen. "Maybe we can find something to do together when you get your homework done tonight?"

Brycen offered a subtle shrug as he placed a couple of pancakes on his plate and doused them with syrup. She reached for the bottle of syrup and followed suit, covering her pancakes with the golden brown liquid.

Her son was deep in thought, tapping his fork against the syrup-covered pancakes. She encouraged him to eat because there wasn't much time before the bus arrived.

"How's the calf supposed to eat without her mom?"

Ashley set her fork down, her son's concern for the calf needing her attention. "She'll need to be bottle fed throughout the day."

Brycen studied his plate before asking, "But won't she miss her mom?"

Ashley thought about it for a minute, unsure of

how to answer her son's question. She didn't doubt animals grieved loss, but the last thing she wanted was for her son to feel sorry for the calf.

"I'm sure she will, just like we miss the ones we love," Ashley said. She chose her words carefully, knowing love and loss was a touchy subject for both her and Brycen. "But it helps when we have others there by our side to see us through it. Sweet Pea will have plenty of us to help her."

Brycen's brows furrowed as a pained expression crossed his face. "She's kind of going through what I did after losing Dad."

It pained Ashley to see her son hurting. Grieving the loss of a loved one was a long process. Filling the gaping hole in their hearts seemed to be their biggest challenge, and coping with the loss got more difficult before it got easier.

Ashley's thoughts trailed off to a time before she knew about love and loss. A time that seemed more like a dream now that she'd gone through the nightmare of losing Colin. No matter how often she'd prayed for the strength to get through it, she never felt she was strong enough.

"Do you think he's proud of me?"

Brycen's question jolted her from her thoughts. "Of course he's proud of you. He was always proud of you," she said while hoping to find the right words. "You were his number one fan, as he was yours. You two were one and the same, and a team like no other."

"I miss him."

"Oh, Bry," Ashley said, scooting closer to him. She reached out and pulled him into a warm embrace. She didn't know what to say to make her son's pain go away, but she would do her best to comfort him. "I miss him, too. He loved us so much…"

She embraced her son, assuring him that no matter what, Colin would be there with them. As long as they carried him in their hearts and their memories never faded, he would always be there.

A knock, followed by Allie's voice announcing her arrival, pulled Brycen out of Ashley's arms. Her heart ached as Brycen wiped away the tears streaming down his face. If she could take away his pain, she would in a heartbeat without the slightest hesitation.

"That's Allie," Brycen announced, shoving a half-eaten pancake into his mouth. Ashley told him to be careful, so he didn't choke as she made her way to the door.

Ashley opened the door and greeted Allie with a "good morning." Allie stood on the porch with bright blue eyes, bouncing blonde curls, and a backpack strapped over her shoulders. "Come on in," Ashley offered as she held open the door and allowed Allie to walk into the house. "He's just finishing up with breakfast and then he'll be ready."

Without pausing, Allie raced to the kitchen and greeted Brycen with a hug. "Do you know what day it is?"

The excitement radiated from the young girl as Brycen tried to figure out the answer to her question. She didn't give him long to think about it before blurting out, "It's field trip day!"

Brycen shot a look at Ashley, but she just smiled. The kids were a few grades apart in school, so it only made sense that Allie would have a field trip Brycen knew nothing about.

"Allie, I think it's just your class that's going on the field trip, isn't it?"

Allie fiddled with the zipper on her winter coat. A soft pout formed on her lips as she thought about Ashley's question. "I thought Brycen could come with us."

"Oh, hon, I'm sure there will be other trips that the two of you can enjoy together," Ashley said, trying her best to reassure the young girl. "Maybe when it gets warmer outside, we can have a picnic."

Allie's eyes lit up at the idea as she announced, "I like picnics! Maybe my mom and Drew can come, too!"

"Of course," Ashley said with a smile on her face. The young girl's excitement was contagious. It put a smile on Brycen's face as well. "It will be a picnic for everyone here at the Dixon Ranch."

"Brycen, let's go," Allie said, tugging on Brycen's arm and leading him to the door. "The bus will be here any minute."

Brycen stopped at the door and looked up at Ashley. The pained expression she'd witnessed a few minutes ago was long gone as he offered her a soft smile. She wrapped her arms around him, hugging him before planting a kiss on the top of his head. "I love you, Bry."

"Love you too, Mom."

He slid his feet into his winter boots before grabbing his backpack and heading out the door. Allie trailed after him, calling out for him to wait up for her.

As the kids made their way down the gravel road, a four wheeler made its way toward Ashley's house. Ashley stayed on the porch as Blake approached the front yard.

He stopped the four wheeler at the bottom of the porch steps and climbed off. "Good morning," he called out as he walked up the front steps to greet her. He was wearing his usual—denim jeans and a long sleeved flannel.

"Good morning," Ashley replied with a weary smile. "What brings you this way?"

Blake lifted his cowboy hat and ran a hand through his hair as he leaned against the railing of her front steps. "Ma's not too keen on keeping the calf in the laundry room," he stated with a slight grin. "She says it's hard to get any work done around there with a calf calling out for attention."

Ashley let out a light chuckle. She could see how impossible it would be for Mama Dixon not to find herself distracted by the small calf.

"I was thinking about moving her to the calving barn," Blake said. His eyes focused on Ashley. She raised a brow, wondering if he wanted her to help with that task. "Do you have a minute or two to give me a hand?"

Ashley had yet to finish eating her breakfast, but she could always find something to munch on later if she got too hungry. "Let me get things put away and then I'll go with you."

She turned toward the door and waited for Blake to follow her inside. "Would you like a cup of coffee while I clean up the kitchen?"

"A woman after my heart," Blake said with a cheesy grin. "I'll never turn coffee down."

"Great," Ashley said as she made her way over to the fresh-brewed pot of coffee. She'd started the coffee while cooking and had yet to grab a cup for herself. She poured a cup for Blake before helping herself to a cup as well. "Here you go."

She slid the coffee across the counter in front of him as his eyes scanned the uneaten breakfast at the table. "Looks like you haven't finished your breakfast."

Ashley hadn't had the time to eat, given the circumstances of comforting a hurting child. "We had a rough start this morning," she explained as she cleared the table. "Brycen is having a hard time with the calf losing its mother…"

Her words trailed off before telling Blake too much. He'd mentioned losing his father, which made sense why she hadn't met him when she first arrived at the ranch. Her thoughts shifted to their conversation from the previous night, and she thought about how Blake could help Brycen cope with the loss of his father.

"I'm sure he's struggling more with it now, given his situation," Blake stated as he took a drink of coffee. Ashley scraped the uneaten food into the garbage as she focused on getting things cleaned up and settled before helping with the calf. "Does he mention his father quite a bit?"

Ashley paused while she gave Blake's question some thought. There had been a time when her son talked about Colin shortly after experiencing the loss. It didn't happen all that often as of late, only when things prompted him to reflect on his loss.

"Every now and then, he will talk about his father and the things he misses the most about him," Ashley said. She kept her eyes focused on the task at hand as she placed the dirty dishes in the sink. Talking to Blake seemed too easy, a little too natural. "Sometimes I find it hard to comfort him. Say the right things. We both miss Colin something terrible, but I'd like to think we're coping with it the best we can."

She sat down at the table, setting her coffee mug down in front of her. Blake nodded as he focused on her, and she wondered if perhaps she'd said too much. The two of them shared some kind of connection with each other. The last thing she wanted was for Blake to think she was leading him on. She wasn't sure if she was ready for a relationship, and she didn't know how all of that would affect Brycen if she and Blake started dating.

"Maybe I can talk to him," Blake suggested. He kept his eyes on Ashley as he said, "I can take him to the spot I used to visit when I was younger. A spot down by the creek where I spent a lot of time while coping with the loss of my father."

Ashley liked the idea of Brycen having someone to talk to besides her. He needed someone who understood the emotions he was feeling. Not that Ashley couldn't relate as she'd lost her own parents, but she'd been an adult by the time she had to deal with their loss.

"I think that might do him some good." Ashley traced the edge of the mug with her thumb, keeping her eyes focused on something other than Blake. "I'd thought about therapy, but I've been putting it off. It's been two years."

Blake stayed silent, but he nodded along as she explained, "I don't know why it's so hard to make the call. I guess I just figured we had each other to get us through it, and one day it would all be okay."

"Time heals all things," Blake said as he studied her. "Or at least that's what they say. I can't say that I wholeheartedly agree with that statement. I mean, sure, it gets easier as the time goes on, but there's always going to be that void in my life… that hole in my heart."

Ashley understood what that felt like. She missed her parents something fierce. There wasn't a day that went by where she didn't long to pick up the phone and hear her mother's voice again. Losing someone you love never gets easier, no matter how many you lose along the way.

"I'll talk to him," Blake stated matter-of-factly. "Maybe while you're working with Doc this afternoon, I'll wait for Brycen to get off the bus and take him for a bit. It shouldn't be too cold by the time four o'clock rolls around."

Ashley liked that idea. The thought of having someone Brycen could talk to eased her worried mind. "I think that sounds wonderful."

"Okay," Blake said as he pushed back his chair from the table and stood. He held out a hand, offering to help Ashley to her feet. She happily accepted his offer and smiled with a grateful heart. "Let's see to the calf and get her settled in the barn. I'm sure she's more than ready for her next bottle."

Ashley followed Blake to the door, slipping on a pair of shoes before walking outside. They made their way to the four wheeler, and Blake motioned for her to climb on behind him. She swung a leg over and grasped Blake's flannel shirt as he guided them back toward the main house.

She wasn't too sure what to expect when it came time to feed the calf, but after getting Sweet Pea to the barn and settled on straw and extra bedding, she realized the process was easier than she'd expected.

"How often does she need to eat? Is it as often as a newborn baby?"

Ashley wrapped an arm around the calf and held the large bottle in the other. She'd never bottle fed an animal before, but there was a first time for everything.

"Not as often as one would think," Blake stated as he found a spot to sit down next to Ashley. "We'll put her on a feeding schedule that will allow her to eat two to three bottles a day."

Ashley raised a brow and studied Blake for a minute before asking, "Only two or three?"

"Yep, for the most part," he said. "Calves only eat about eight percent of their birth weight, at least until they're eight weeks old. It's hard to believe, isn't it?"

Ashley nodded as she held the bottle for the calf. "Nothing like a newborn baby, then. Brycen ate a couple of ounces every few hours."

Blake chuckled as he shook his head. "I'm afraid that would be feeding the calf a bit too much."

"Makes sense," Ashley said with a half-laugh. "Kind of."

Blake shook his head as he kept his eye on her and the calf. "You'll get the hang of things around here."

She wasn't sure when that would be, because her grandfather still had a lot to show her. There were only so many hours in a day, and it seemed she spent most of them learning only a thing or two about the ranch, which seemed not nearly enough. When she wasn't learning by her grandfather's side, she was with Blake and Brycen.

Ashley passed Blake the bottle and allowed him to take over the feeding. The man had a soft spot for animals. She leaned back and watched his interaction with the calf, letting herself get lost in thoughts of the future and what life on the ranch would be like if she stayed there forever.

CHAPTER FOURTEEN

Blake spent most of the day to himself as he cleaned up the office and prepared a space for Ashley to work on the books whenever she found the time. He wouldn't deny the fact that he was more than thankful she accepted his offer, knowing it would give him time to focus on running the ranch and less time worrying about the finances. It would also give him more time to spend with her, as a part of him craved getting to know her better. There was something about her that had hooked and reeled him in, refusing to let him focus on what needed to be done around the ranch.

He thought about the conversation he'd had with Ashley about Brycen. The ten-year-old reminded Blake a lot of himself when he was that age. Losing his father had been a hard pill to swallow. It was something Blake had learned to deal with from day to day. If he were to be honest, he still struggled to cope with the loss, even now.

He'd offered to have a talk with Brycen, hoping it would give the boy some comfort knowing he wasn't alone in dealing with loss. He wouldn't push the subject, but would be ready to talk about it if the opportunity presented itself.

Right now, he focused on getting the office situated and settled. He still had some time before the bus dropped Brycen off at the ranch.

Blake grabbed the folder Ashley had been looking over before being pulled out of the office to ward off the pack of wolves. The thought of calling Curt and having him meet at the office crossed his mind as he looked over the paid invoices and balanced each one with the spreadsheet.

Blake might have paid for something that Curt had taken care of prior to heading back to Maple Glen. Taking over the ranch had been unexpected and hadn't given Blake a chance to get his feet wet before diving in. It had been a lot to take on with such a short notice.

Blake spent the next few hours flipping through the papers and trying his best to find the discrepancy. From the looks of it, Curt had run a tight ship with bookkeeping until late December, around the time of his move to Maple Glen. That was when he'd hired the accountant to step in and take over in his absence. His uncle had trusted the woman to keep things under control and the bills paid while he figured things out back home.

Blake thought about calling the accountant, but dismissed the idea no sooner than it had crossed his mind. He needed to work through the files and try to figure it out on his own before reaching out to the accountant or his uncle.

After spending a few hours after lunch in the office, Blake placed a page flag where he left off and closed the folder. The bus would drop Brycen off any minute, and he gladly accepted the break from numbers.

He grabbed his cowboy hat from the edge of his desk and made his way out the door. The mid-afternoon sun had melted the snow, leaving mud holes in its place while providing unexpected warmth in the early weeks of November.

Blake made his way down the driveway, meeting the bus just as it stopped near the edge. Brycen and Allie raced each other off the bus and ran toward Blake. Allie screeched to a halt in front of Blake, a wide smile on her face. "Nana and I are going to bake cookies!"

"Alright," Blake said with a slight nod. Allie gave him a quick hug before racing off toward the main house.

"Girls," Brycen mumbled under his breath, which gave Blake a pleasant laugh.

"Tell me about it," Blake said with a playful grin. "Just wait until you have your first girlfriend."

Brycen shook his head and waved his arms in front of him. "No way. Not happening."

Brycen stuck his tongue out and pointed a finger into his mouth while making a gagging sound. "Ick."

"One day you'll change your mind," Blake said, knowing the boy had no idea what it was like falling head over heels in love with a girl. It was only a matter of time before the young boy had his first crush. Blake laughed it off as they started up the driveway and headed toward the stables. "What do you say we grab Chance and head to the creek? I already told your mother that I was planning to hang out with you for a bit after school."

Brycen's eyes lit up as he let out a loud, "Yes!"

"If I didn't know any better, I'd think you've been waiting for this moment," Blake teased, nudging the boy with an elbow as they walked along the muddy gravel.

"Drew says he's going to give me riding lessons, but it won't be anytime soon," Brycen said, a disappointed look crossing his face. Blake felt bad for Drew getting the kid's hopes up just to make him wait.

"Drew's been pretty busy with training horses,"

Blake said. He was thankful for the supplemental income for the ranch. "Not to mention helping Shyann rehabilitate the abandoned horses she's found since moving onto the ranch."

Brycen kept pace with Blake as they headed for the stables. "What does rehabilitate mean?"

"It means that she helps get horses healthy again."

"Where does she find the horses?"

"She finds them all over. Some people can't take care of horses like they think they can," Blake explained as he pushed open the barn door and motioned for Brycen to go ahead of him. He led Brycen toward Chance's stall and said, "Taking care of horses is an enormous responsibility that some people aren't prepared for. There's more to taking care of them besides feeding and riding them."

Brycen offered an understanding nod as Blake pulled a few baby carrots from his pocket. He handed a couple to Brycen after offering one to Chance. "Go ahead and give him one. Let him get used to you before we take him out," Blake said as he stood near the wooden stall and watched Brycen interact with the horse. "Chance is the horse that Drew worked with for a few months. He broke him in and—"

Brycen stopped feeding the horse and looked at Blake with wide eyes. "He broke him? What did he break?"

Blake held back a laugh as Brycen inspected the

horse through the wooden slats of the gate. "No, not that kind of break," Blake explained. "'Breaking a horse' just means training them and getting them used to people. He spent a lot of time with Chance and got him used to interacting with humans."

"Oh, well, I guess that's a good thing then," Brycen said with a laugh. "I thought it meant he broke his leg or something."

Blake shook his head with a light chuckle as he reached for Chance's saddle. "What do you say we get him saddled up and ready to ride?"

"Let's do it!"

"Safety first." Blake grabbed a riding helmet from a nearby hook and handed it to Brycen. Without hesitation or argument, Brycen slipped the helmet over his head and latched it underneath his chin.

Proud of the boy for accepting the helmet, Blake strapped the saddle onto Chance and adjusted the reins before climbing into the saddle. He reached out a hand to Brycen and helped the young boy climb into the saddle behind him. "You'll want to hang on tight," Blake said as he guided Chance out of the barn. "The ride might get a little rough on the way to the creek."

Blake waited until Brycen wrapped his arms around him and held on tight before guiding Chance away from the barn and toward the creek.

The afternoon sun made for a muddy ride, but Blake didn't mind. It felt good to be on the back of the horse without a job waiting for him. He would always make time for a carefree ride to the water's edge. Today was no different, except for the fact he'd brought someone with him this time.

"When I was your age, I would ride down to the creek and sit there for hours, skipping rocks into the water," Blake said as Chance walked at a slow and steady pace. "It gave me a break from the day-to-day routine."

"Did you have to go to school?"

"I sure did," Blake said matter-of-factly. "Everyone has to go to school if they want to learn a thing or two."

"But did you like going?" Brycen's voice was almost a soft whisper in the wind as they headed for the creek. Blake had a hard time hearing him, but heard what the boy wasn't saying loud and clear.

"From what I can remember, I enjoyed going just to see my friends," Blake said with a light chuckle. "But I suppose I learned a thing or two I wouldn't have if I hadn't gone to school."

Silence surrounded them, and Blake wondered what Brycen was thinking. He could only imagine it hadn't been a smooth transition from one school to another. He hated to think about how hard that would be for a kid at any age.

Blake accepted the silence as he led Chance to the creek. Coming to a stop by an old tree, he helped

Brycen out of the saddle and onto the ground before climbing off the horse himself. Brycen slid the helmet off of his head and set it against an old tree stump. "I liked my old school better than this one."

Brycen's statement caught Blake off guard as he tied off the reins and made sure Chance couldn't go anywhere. "I'm sure moving here and starting over hasn't been easy."

Brycen shook his head and shrugged. "I miss my friends."

"I'm sure they miss you, too," Blake said. He picked up a few rocks along the edge of the creek and offered one to Brycen. "But if I didn't know any better, I'd say you're making some new ones here at the new school?"

Brycen thought about it for a minute before saying, "Yeah, but it's not the same."

There was no doubt in Blake's mind that the young boy was struggling to adjust to moving to a new town and starting a new school. He could hear the sadness in the boy's voice as he talked about his old school and how things used to be.

"It must have been hard to leave everyone behind like that," Blake said as he skipped a rock across the water. He handed Brycen another rock and showed him how to skip it, impressed with the boy's first attempt. "Here, try again. This time, let your wrist relax before you whip the rock into the water."

Brycen practiced a few more times before catching on to the entire process of skipping stones. "See, there's nothing to it. You're a pro at it."

Brycen's face lit up with a smile, and it felt good to see him smile. The talk of leaving his friends behind, starting a new school, and not liking it had put a damper on the boy's mood. Not that Blake could blame him. He'd thought about the changes he'd gone through in life. Sometimes they weren't easy to deal with—including the loss of his father.

"Do you enjoy living here at the ranch?" Blake asked as he watched Brycen skip stones one after another into the creek. Thankfully, the temperatures hadn't dropped low enough to freeze the stream. "With your ma and great-grandpa?"

"And Allie, too."

Blake smiled at the mention of Allie. "And Allie, too."

"It's a lot of fun here, but I still miss my old house and friends," Brycen admitted. "I just wish we never had to move."

Blake didn't want to push the subject, so he kept quiet and listened as Brycen opened up about life in the city. He talked about school and his friends. The sports he'd taken part in and how much he missed them.

"Sometimes things happen in life that are out of our control, buddy. Things change in a blink of an eye and leave us no choice but to change right along with them."

Brycen tossed another rock into the water and watched it skip across the stream.

"I've always lived on the ranch, but things haven't always been easy around here," Blake said. "Growing up, I thought I had it made. I had all kinds of friends, I had my family... I had a lot to be thankful for even when things got hard."

Brycen looked over at him now, listening as Blake talked about his life growing up on the ranch. Blake hesitated a few times, making sure he didn't say the wrong thing. He chose his words carefully, and when given the opportunity, he opened up about his own loss.

"That all changed when I lost my father, though," Blake said. He took a minute to ponder his words before continuing, "Everything changed in a blink of an eye, and I don't remember much other than how sad I was even though I didn't understand much about death."

"Your dad died, too?" Brycen asked. The kid gave Blake a sympathetic look of understanding when Blake nodded. "How old were you? Were you eight?"

"Nope, but close," Blake stated. "I was six."

"Six?" Brycen replied with a shocked look on his face. He looked down at the ground and kicked a few rocks. "I was eight when my dad died."

Blake's heart ached for the young boy, knowing just how hard losing his father had been. "I'm sorry," Blake said, not sure what else he could say.

"It's okay," Brycen said. "He's not in pain anymore, and Mom says that he's still with us in our hearts."

Blake tried his best to keep his emotions in check as he cleared his throat. His thoughts drifted to Ashley and what she had gone through right along with Brycen. He felt like a heel for even thinking about wanting something more with Ashley and Brycen after everything they'd gone through.

"She says that he'll always be with us as long as we carry him in our hearts and our memories never fade," Brycen said. He looked up at the sky and said, "I know he's watching over us from up there in heaven."

Blake nodded, agreeing with the young boy. "Yeah, I'd like to think my dad's up there, too, smiling down on us when he's not busy riding bulls."

Brycen shot a surprised look at Blake and asked, "They can ride bulls in heaven?"

Blake swallowed hard as he thought of what to say. "Well, I'm not a hundred percent sure what it's like in heaven, as I've never been there," he said with a slight chuckle, "but from what I've read in the Bible, there's a lot to look forward to when our job here on earth is done."

Brycen offered a quick nod, accepting Blake's explanation. "Do you think our dads are proud of us?"

Blake choked back the emotion the kid's question stirred. He picked up a few rocks and handed one to Brycen before tossing them into the creek. There had been a few times, more often than not, when Blake thought about his father and couldn't help but wonder if the man was proudly watching over Blake and his brothers as they worked the ranch.

"Mom says Dad was always proud of me," Brycen said, without waiting too long for Blake to answer him. "I'd like to think he's still proud of me... I just miss him."

"I miss my dad, too, bud," Blake said as he reached out and wrapped an arm around the kid's shoulders. He didn't have the right words to say, but he wanted Brycen to know he wasn't alone. He had several people who cared about him and loved him that would look after him. "Losing someone you love and care about never gets easier, but knowing you're not alone makes all the difference."

Brycen nodded and leaned into Blake's side. Blake squeezed the boy's shoulder, offering him comfort the best way he knew how.

"You can always talk to me when things get hard, okay?" Blake asked while giving the boy another gentle squeeze against him. "Anytime you need to talk, day or night, I'll be right here."

"Okay," Brycen said as he stepped out of Blake's embrace. "Thanks."

Blake shook off the emotions running through him. He'd gotten softer over the years, and seeing how much Brycen was hurting only made it that much worse.

"What do you say we head back to the barn? I'm sure your mom and Gramps are looking for us, and it's just about time for supper, anyway."

With that, Brycen skipped one more rock into the creek before sliding the helmet over his head. Blake climbed into the saddle and reached out a hand to help Brycen into the saddle behind him. It had felt good to talk with Brycen, and it felt even better knowing they'd bonded. Blake's heart broke for the young boy, but that would never stop him from caring too much.

CHAPTER FIFTEEN

"If I didn't know any better, I'd like to think that Blake's coming around and liking the idea of having you and Brycen here at the ranch."

Her grandfather studied her as he waited for her reaction. Ashley had talked little about the progression of her and Blake's relationship.

"It seems that he has taken Brycen under his wing," her grandfather stated as they focused their attention on Blake and Brycen riding in from the creek. "It'll do Brycen some good to spend some time with Blake. Those two have a lot more in common other than what meets the eye."

Ashley couldn't argue with her grandfather. She'd witnessed Blake's connection with Brycen firsthand. Blake had taken it upon himself to look after Brycen.

It was almost as though he stepped in when Ashley needed him the most, and because of that, she had seen the softer side of Blake she once thought didn't exist.

"I think the two of you are going to be just fine," her grandfather said. His words pulled Ashley from her thoughts as she watched Blake and Brycen make their way toward them. Blake had his arm wrapped around Brycen's shoulders, pulling him in close as they walked down the muddy driveway. Laughter and excitement rang out from her little boy, and it melted Ashley's heart to witness their interaction. "See what I mean?"

Her grandfather offered Ashley a slight nudge with his elbow and gave her a knowing look. Ashley felt the connection deep down, knowing it was good for them to have someone like Blake in their life.

"Mom! Grandpa!" Brycen called out as he raced to the front porch of the main house. "Blake took me for a ride down to the creek and taught me how to skip rocks."

"Is that right?" Ashley's grandfather said with a grin.

"I'm going to find Allie and tell her all about it," Brycen said as he raced up the stairs behind them. Ashley turned and called out, "Don't forget to wash up for supper."

Her grandfather cracked a knowing smile as

Ashley and Blake exchanged glances. He stepped back and walked up the porch steps. "I'll leave the two of you alone for a minute," he said as he reached for the railing. "I'll see you inside."

Ashley waited for her grandfather to walk into the house before turning her attention back to Blake. He combed a steady hand through his dark hair and replaced his cowboy hat on top of his head. "How'd things go with Brycen?"

Blake stepped closer now, closing the distance between them as he motioned for her to follow him up the steps. He sat down on the porch swing and patted the empty spot next to him, leaving her no choice but to take it.

"He's holding onto a lot of hurt, but I think talking about it is going to help him," Blake said. "I think it helps him to know that I've been there, too. He seemed to relax a bit more when I told him about losing my father when I was six."

Ashley nodded along as Blake talked about spending time with Brycen at the creek. He'd made it fun and interactive for Brycen while he prepared to have a deep conversation. "Thank you," Ashley whispered. "That means a lot to me. Having someone Brycen can talk to while knowing he isn't alone."

"He knows he's never been alone," Blake said as he placed his hand on top of hers. She glanced down at his hand on hers, wondering when they'd crossed the line between strangers and something more. She tried her best to calm the awakened flutter of butterflies as she focused on what Blake was saying instead. "He's always had you. I think having me talk to him has helped him understand that someone else feels the same pain he does. Understands the hurt that he feels, ya know?"

Ashley swallowed past the lump in her throat. She'd tried her best to help Brycen cope with the loss of his father, while trying to cope with the loss as well. She liked to think they'd managed just fine, but maybe she'd been wrong? Maybe she should have listened to the experts and sought therapy for him... and for her.

"Hey," Blake said. He tugged at her hand as he focused his eyes on hers. "Where'd you go just now?"

Ashley held back the stinging tears in her eyes. She refused to break now. She'd come so far on her own. She wasn't weak. The last thing she wanted was for Blake to see her cry. She was stronger than that. She'd pulled it together time and time again as she remained strong for the both of them.

"Ash," Blake whispered, leaning closer to her now as she tried her best to keep her emotions in check. "It's okay."

He traced his thumb along the side of her cheek. She leaned her face into his hand as she stared at him. Concerned eyes stared back at her, willing her to tell him what was bothering her. "Everything's going to be okay," Blake assured her as he wrapped an arm around her and pulled her against him. "Brycen's a strong kid. He's got a heart the size of Montana. It might've been broken a time or two, but there's nothing time and love can't heal."

Ashley leaned into Blake and warmed against him. She liked to believe there was hope for overcoming the loss she and Brycen had experienced. That there was hope to fill the void in her heart from the loss of her husband.

Blake held her close, wrapping her in his arms and comforting her with his words. He placed a kiss on the top of her head as he held onto her. Ashley listened to the beat of his heart as he combed his fingers through her hair.

"You might have been alone before now," Blake said, his voice low. "But you have me now, Ash. I'll always be here for you and Brycen. No matter what."

Ashley nodded as tears filled her eyes. She wasn't sure how or when they had crossed that line to something more, but she wouldn't fight it. With Blake's muscular arms wrapped around her, holding her close to him, she felt comfort and security. Like she could relax and let everything she'd been carrying by herself fall off her shoulders.

She looked up, meeting Blake's eyes as he looked down at her. "Thank you."

He ran a thumb along her cheek, drying the tears that had betrayed her and streamed down her face no matter how hard she fought to hold them back. Their eyes locked on one another as Blake leaned in closer, closing the little distance they had between them. His warm breath lingered between them as his eyes searched hers, looking for a sign that she wanted something more. She tilted her head and her breath hitched, catching in her throat as his lips met with hers.

The slamming of the screen door jolted them away from each other as Brycen stepped onto the front porch and caught them. "Mom, are you guys coming in for sup—" His words cut off, caught off guard as he looked from Ashley to Blake.

Ashley righted herself, quickly wiping any sign of tears from her cheeks as she reeled from their first kiss. She wasn't sure what to say to Brycen as he stood in the doorway with a look of surprise on his face.

"Yeah, hon," Ashley said, standing from the porch swing and making her way to Brycen's side. "We were just getting ready to come inside to eat."

Ashley watched as awareness of what had just happened between the two of them cross her son's face. The look of wanting to ask questions mixed with uncertainty and despair stirred in Brycen's eyes before he backed away and ran down the porch steps and took off toward their cabin.

"Brycen, wait," Ashley called after him as she left the porch. Her heart sank as she chased after her son. "Brycen."

She hurried after her son with Blake close behind. She should have known better than to leave Brycen in the dark about their budding relationship.

Ashley took the front steps two at a time until she reached the front door. Without catching her breath, she walked inside and followed Brycen up to his room. "Brycen," she said, trying her best to get her son to acknowledge her efforts. It was a little too late, she knew that, but she needed him to talk with her.

The spacious loft provided her easy access to her son without having to worry about talking through a door. Brycen curled himself into a ball and faced the wall, looking away from her. Her heart sank at the devastating look that crossed her son's face. She'd known the day would come when she would have this conversation, but if she were to be honest, she hadn't expected it to happen so soon. Blake was a decent man, and she couldn't deny how he made her feel.

Heavy footsteps sounded on the stairs behind her. Blake leaned against the wall as she tried her best to talk with Brycen.

Ashley walked into her son's room and sat on the edge of his bed. She rubbed a hand over his back to comfort him. He squirmed out of her reach as he sank closer to the wall.

"Bry," she spoke softly, "let's talk, okay?"

A quick shake of his head told her she wouldn't get too far in the conversation.

She inched closer to him, leaving him no room to pull away. "Honey, come here," she said as she tugged on his arm in an attempt to sit him up next to her. He burrowed his head underneath the pillows and let out a soft whimper. It pained her to see him hurting. She should have known better than to let something happen between her and Blake. Everything happened so fast… one minute they were carrying on in conversation, and the next thing she knew, talking was the furthest thing from her thoughts.

"You don't love Dad anymore."

Her son's words would have shattered her heart if it hadn't already been in a million tiny pieces.

"That's not true," she said as she swallowed past the lump forming in her throat. "I loved your dad very much, and nothing will ever change the love I have for him."

"You're lying," Brycen said as he sat up and pulled his blanket into his lap. Ashley tried to comfort him, but he pulled away every time she got close. "You don't love Dad, and I know it."

"I'll always love your father." Ashley fought back the tears that threatened to escape as her emotions consumed her. She didn't know what to say to make Brycen understand. Her love for Colin would never fade. Colin held a special place in her heart that she would hold on to for the rest of her life.

"Then why'd you kiss Blake?" Brycen's bottom lip quivered as he asked her the question she didn't have the answer to. She had fallen for Blake, that things had evolved quicker than she would have liked. But none of that would make sense to a ten-year-old who was still grieving the loss of his father. "I saw you kiss him."

Ashley took a deep breath and released it slowly, willing herself to find the words to say. She reached forward, taking Brycen's hands in hers. "Listen, honey," she said as she slid closer to him. "I loved your father very much, and nothing will ever change the love I have for him. He was everything I ever wanted, and he provided us with so much more than I could have ever imagined. I'll always love your father. He'll always be in my heart."

"Then why are you trying to replace him?"

Brycen's eyes filled with tears as she clung to his hands. Ashley tried her best to see everything from her son's point of view, but failed miserably. "I'm not trying to replace him," she stated matter-of-factly, praying for her son to believe her. "No one could ever replace your father, Brycen. Your father will always be your father no matter what."

Brycen wiped away the tears streaming down his cheeks with the back of his hand as he thought about what she'd told him. "Do you love Blake like you loved Dad?"

"Love is a very strong word," Ashley said. She struggled to find the right words to say, knowing Blake was standing there behind them. She wanted her son to know there was a possibility that she could end up loving Blake, but for right now, she was playing it safe.

"But I thought you only kiss the people you love?"

She was failing to make her son understand what had transpired between her and Blake. She found it more difficult to tell Brycen how she truly felt about Blake when she wasn't so sure herself.

"That's true," Ashley said. "But sometimes it just happens when you like someone, too."

Retreating footsteps sounded on the stairs behind her as she tried her best to explain everything to her son. Blake was no longer standing behind them. The latching of the front door was proof that he'd left the house.

She turned her attention back to Brycen, struggling to make sense of the mix of emotions running through her. Ashley didn't regret kissing Blake. The only regret was not being able to prepare Brycen for what he'd witnessed on the front porch. If she'd been given more time, she could have talked with Brycen and explained her and Blake's budding relationship before feelings were hurt.

"I like Blake, too, Mom." Brycen leaned back against his headboard and fiddled with the edge of his blanket. "He's super nice, and he made me feel better after our talk at the creek."

Ashley wasn't sure what to say to that. The heaviness in the room seemed to dissipate around them as Brycen opened up about his feelings for Blake. "I can tell that he cares about us, Mom. Just like Dad used to."

Ashley released a slow breath, willing herself to take it one thing at a time. She couldn't expect her son to understand the dynamics of a relationship and how falling in love happened. He was still a young child who was coping with the loss of his father.

"Yes, I believe Blake cares about us," she admitted. "I care a lot about Blake, too, but that doesn't mean that he'll ever replace your father, okay?"

Brycen nodded as Ashley wiped away the stray tears from his cheek. "Even if I love Blake someday soon, I will always love your father. No one will ever take his place in my heart. He's there forever, okay?"

Brycen offered a quick nod again and leaned into Ashley. He wrapped his arms around her and hugged her as he melted against her. "I love you, Mom."

"I love you, too, baby."

CHAPTER SIXTEEN

Blake walked the short distance back to the main house, knowing he would get twenty questions when his family realized Ashley and Brycen weren't with him. He hadn't meant for the evening to fall apart as it had. He should have known better than to kiss Ashley.

There were a lot of things he should have known better before doing, but he hadn't thought twice when it came to Ashley. He should have known things were going too well. Almost too good to be true.

"Where's Ash and Brycen?" Mama Dixon questioned no sooner than Blake stepped into the house.

"They went back to their house for the evening," Blake said, keeping his voice low. The last thing he needed was for his brothers or the ranch hands to catch wind that something happened between the two of them. They'd already given him plenty of grief about not settling down and scaring the women off. "Brycen wasn't feeling well."

His mother raised a brow and studied him for a minute. Blake knew she was about to call his bluff when she said, "He seemed just fine a bit ago."

"Well, maybe he ate too much candy or something. I don't know." Blake offered a subtle shrug, not sure what else he could say to stop his mother's line of questioning.

Mama Dixon shook her head as she scooped food onto an empty plate before handing it off to Blake. "That boy hadn't touched a lick of candy when he was here. He was more than ready to eat supper while waiting for the two of you to come inside."

His mother shot him a knowing look, silently warning him she knew better. Blake thanked her for the food and walked into the dining room. He pulled up a chair at the table and prepared to eat without saying another word.

The only problem was that he knew better than to think he'd get by without someone asking more questions.

"Where's Brycen and Ashley?" Allie asked as she shoved a forkful of spaghetti into her mouth.

"I don't think Brycen's feeling too well," Blake lied, knowing there was a possibility it would come back to bite him later on. "Ashley took him home to relax for the evening."

Much to his relief, Allie let it rest and kindly accepted his little white lie for the time being. Blake could have told them all the truth... that he'd rushed things with Ashley and they both should have known better. *He* should have known better. Who was he to think that the two of them could have a relationship, anyway? Not to mention Brycen. The boy was still coping with the loss of his father. Blake had seen the look on the boy's face when he'd caught them on the front porch swing.

"I still find that hard to believe," Mama Dixon said as she sat down at the other end of the table. "He seemed just fine when he was here. He was ready to eat supper before going out to grab you and Ashley."

Several nods rounded the table as his mother tried her best to figure out what happened in the little time Brycen had been on the front porch. Blake didn't look up. Instead, he kept his eyes on his plate as he spun his fork in the heaping pile of spaghetti.

"Are you sure Brycen didn't catch the two of you—"

"No," Blake said in a tense tone. He eyed Drew, warning him to drop it. Before Blake could come up with an excuse, the front door opened and Ashley followed Brycen inside.

Blake's eyes met hers, and she offered an apologetic smile. He dropped his eyes back to his plate and continued to eat while the rest of his family doted on their return.

"How are you feeling, Brycen?" Mama Dixon asked, motioning for the two of them to join the table. Brycen's brows scrunched in confusion as he looked from Mama Dixon back to his mother.

"I feel fine," Brycen said with a slight shrug as he sat down at the table next to Allie.

"Uncle Blake said you weren't feeling good," Allie said as she prepared to shove another forkful of spaghetti into her sauce-covered mouth.

Ashley raised a brow as she studied Blake from across the room. She made her way over to the empty chair next to Blake and sat down, not giving him time to assist her.

"Nope, I'm fine," Brycen stated once again as he scooped spaghetti onto his plate with a smile. "Spaghetti is my favorite."

The young boy and Allie carried on a conversation about spaghetti while Ashley sat next to Blake.

"How's Miss Sweet Pea doing?" Mama Dixon asked as she studied Blake.

"She's good," Blake said as he twisted his fork in the spaghetti. "We've been bottle feeding her for the last few days, and she's putting on some weight."

Blake kept the chatter to a minimum. He hated to think about the conversation he was planning to have with Ashley after supper. They would have to take a step back. Call it quits. He should have known better than to fall for an employee at the ranch—regardless of how normal it had felt.

"That's good," Mama Dixon said, appeased with the bit of information Blake provided. He prayed for the awkwardness to leave the room, but knew better than to think it would. He was the one making it awkward by not conversing the way he usually did at suppertime. "Ashley," Mama Dixon said as she turned toward her. "Do you think your grandfather's going to retire as the community vet anytime soon?"

Blake knew his mother was just making conversation. An attempt to limit the awkwardness surrounding them at the table. Normally, he would have liked to engage in small talk, but not tonight.

"He hasn't said too much to me about retiring," Ashley said, her voice soft. "But that doesn't mean he hasn't thought about it."

"I don't think that old man will ever retire," Drew said with a slight laugh. "He's invested quite a bit of time into his business. I honestly think he loves it too much to give it up just yet."

Blake nodded along with what his brother was saying. He liked to think the old man would stick with it until the day he could no longer physically handle it. But Blake also knew the Dixon Ranch wasn't his only focus. Even though Doc Thompson had given the ranch top priority, he served the entire community of Woodford Creek.

"No way," Garrett said as he set his fork down on his empty plate and wiped his mouth with a napkin. "Doc has a few good years left before he thinks twice about retiring."

Mama Dixon turned her attention back to Ashley and asked, "Do you think you're going to take over for him the day he retires?"

Blake swallowed hard, forcing the last bite of spaghetti down with a gulp of water. "He's not retiring," Blake said with a low growl. "We don't have to worry about any of that just yet."

The entire table fell silent as they looked at Blake. He hadn't meant to get upset about it, but enough was enough. The last thing he wanted to worry about was losing a darn good vet at the ranch. Not to mention, if Ashley were to decide not to stick around long after finishing her internship.

"I've got to get back to work," Blake said, sliding his chair back and grabbing his plate. He walked into the kitchen and scraped his plate before setting it in the sink. "I'll see you all later. Have a good night."

His eyes met Ashley's just before he grabbed his cowboy hat from the hook and walked out the door. He didn't have time to sit around and talk about the future of the ranch when he wasn't sure there would even be a ranch. If he couldn't keep the predators away, or the cattle well fed enough through the winter months, the ranch wouldn't make a profit come spring.

Blake walked out to the barn and thought about how he'd reacted at the table. He wasn't one to bite his tongue all too well, but he also wasn't one to lose his temper, either.

The way Ashley had looked at him tonight, with those warm blue eyes full of concern and uncertainty. Blake didn't have the heart to tell her what was on his mind. He'd do his best to avoid having that conversation for as long as he could. He didn't usually avoid confrontation or squashing a problem when he saw one coming, but it was different with Ashley.

Blake saddled Chance and guided him out of the stall. He needed to make the rounds out in the pasture anyway, which would give him an excuse to avoid having a conversation with Ashley. He tightened the reins and climbed into the saddle once they cleared the barn.

Blake guided Chance through the gate of the pasture as he scanned the property for any sign of predators. There was no doubt in his mind that the pack of wolves would be back for another round, given the opportunity. Not to mention mountain lions and the potential for bears making their way down from the mountains in search of food before hunkering down for winter.

The ranch hands he'd hired since taking over the ranch were good about looking after the herd. Since the first attack of the winter, everyone had been keeping an extra eye on their pregnant cows and moving them into the birthing barn before taking chances of another birth in the pasture.

The chance of a birthing cow being missed was slim to none, but Blake knew it could still happen. No matter how many eyes were on the herd, there was always a chance something was overlooked.

Blake nudged Chance into a full trot as they set out to the outer edge of the property line. The sun was setting just beyond the western edge of the mountains as Blake focused on the herd. He made a few rounds, checking on the herd and scanning the pasture for newborn calves while keeping his eyes on the fence line. There seemed to be no sign of hungry predators nearby, and the herd seemed to be more settled than they had been the other night.

Blake's thoughts went back to the night of the attack. Maybe they'd done enough to scare the pack of wolves off, but he highly doubted it. He thought about Ashley and the way she'd saved the calf. Adrenaline had been running high that night, and

Blake still wasn't sure she realized just how lucky she had been.

Then he thought about their kiss. The way she'd melted into his arms and allowed him to comfort her. No matter how many times he'd told himself to keep his distance, to not get too attached to Ashley and Brycen, he'd done it anyway. He didn't like the way Brycen looked at him after seeing the two of them kiss. He hadn't liked hearing the young boy question his mother, either. Brycen thinking that he was trying to replace his father didn't sit well with Blake.

It was time to pull back the reins and put a stop to whatever hope Blake had of falling in love and having a family of his own. To be honest, he should have known better than to think Ashley and Brycen were ready to move on with their life. Ashley hadn't come to the ranch looking for a relationship or a father for Brycen. Blake should have stepped back and kept his distance from the very beginning. Having Ashley on the ranch was distracting enough without having to worry about overstepping and causing hurt feelings. The last thing he wanted was for Brycen to hate him.

A low growl followed by a deep howl sounded behind Blake as he rode along the fence line. He pulled tight on Chance's reins, halting their trot. Blake scanned the area surrounding the pasture, searching for the leader of the pack, but came up with nothing.

He turned in the saddle, scanning the rest of the woods and looking for any sign of movement along the outer edge of the property. The howling grew closer, echoing in the wide-open space of the mountains surrounding the ranch.

Blake steadied Chance, keeping his eye out for incoming danger. No sooner had the thought of being alone in the wide open pasture crossed his mind than he heard the pounding of hooves and the revving of a four wheeler behind him.

"You could've told us you were coming out here," Mason called out as he got closer on the four wheeler. Garrett was keeping pace next to him on Shyann's horse, Star. "We were wondering where you took off to."

"I needed some fresh air, and figured I'd check on the herd before heading in for the night." Blake hooked a thumb over his shoulder and said, "We've got some howling in the woods behind us. They seem to be moving in closer."

Mason and Garrett scanned the area while Blake came up with a plan. They couldn't risk another attack on their herd. The first attack cost them plenty, and the thought of losing more made Blake sick to his stomach.

"What do you think about moving the herd to the cattle barn tonight?"

It was good to know that Garrett was on the same

page as Blake when it came to protecting the cattle. They should have moved them earlier in the day instead of waiting until nightfall, but that was neither here nor there now.

"Let's round up what we can and head them into the barn," Blake ordered as he took action. "No sense in waiting any longer. It should've been done long before the first attack."

Blake worked with them, rounding up the herd and pushing them toward the smaller lot and cattle barn. There was no telling how long they had before the wolves attempted another attack.

Mason followed nearby on the four wheeler, ready to redirect the cattle who tried to wander as Blake and Garrett drove the herd toward safety. They worked diligently together and took no time to get the cattle settled.

Blake climbed out of the saddle and latched the barn door as he gave everyone a thumbs up. "I'd say they're good for the night. Thanks for the help."

Mason climbed off the four wheeler and scanned the property. They had moved the cattle more than a few hundred feet in record time. "If you want, I can stick around for a bit just to make sure."

Blake liked the idea of having someone to watch over the herd, but he was certain the cattle would be safe for the night. He needed Mason bright and early in the morning to finish mucking stalls and placing fresh bedding in the stalls. Not to mention running into town for feed.

"I think they're good for the night," Blake assured them as he scanned the woods. The howling seemed to have moved away from the ranch, which meant the threat of an attack, though still possible, was minimal. The wolves were moving on. "Thanks for all of your help."

"Anytime," Mason said, slapping Blake on the shoulder before climbing back onto the four wheeler. "I'll see you guys in the morning."

Blake hung back as he watched Mason take off toward the main road that would lead him to his cabin. Garrett climbed out of Star's saddle and met Blake on the ground with a questioning look.

"What are you looking at me like that for?" Blake questioned. "If you've got something to say, just spit it out already."

Garrett kicked the snow-covered ground with the toe of his cowboy boot as Blake waited for him to say whatever he had to say. "What happened tonight between you and Ashley?"

Blake shot him a piercing look, warning his brother not to go there, but Garrett didn't seem to take notice. "I mean, word has it you two were getting pretty close on the front porch."

"That's none of your business," Blake said matter-of-factly. He wasn't the type to kiss and tell, and he certainly wouldn't tell his brother anything.

Garrett seemed to think about it for a minute before saying, "Well, if I didn't know any better, I'd think Brycen caught the two of you kissing and—"

Blake furrowed his brow and shot a look at his brother. The last thing Blake needed tonight was his brother digging for information about him and Ashley. Garrett held up his hands in defense as he took a step back. "Take it easy, bro. I'm just asking what everyone's dying to know."

Blake shook his head. The thought of being the topic of conversation at the dinner table after he'd left the house irked him. If they had something to say, they all could have very well said it while he was there.

"What do you mean by 'everyone'?"

Garrett ran a hand through his hair as he leaned against the side of the barn. "Once you left, Ashley and Brycen took off for home and left us wondering what happened between the two of you," Garrett explained. "You can't tell me nothing happened when we all witnessed how awkward you were acting when Ashley sat down beside you."

Blake thought about that moment when Ashley and Brycen stepped into the house. Their eyes had met for a split second, leaving Blake restless after overhearing her talk with Brycen. If he'd known any better, he wouldn't have followed her. He should have let her tend to Brycen alone. He'd had no business being there.

"Hey," Garrett said as he waved a hand in front of Blake's face. "What's going on in that head of yours?"

"Nothing I can't handle on my own," Blake stated. Telling his brother anything was the last thing Blake wanted to do.

"Whatever you say."

Blake watched as Garrett stepped toward Star and climbed into the saddle. Garrett looked back at Blake and shook his head. "You're a stubborn one, you know that?"

Blake offered a low grunt in response as he walked over to Chance and climbed onto the horse. "I'm not the only one," he assured. "There's plenty of stubbornness around here to last us a lifetime."

Garrett nodded in agreement. "Just promise me you won't do something foolish and wreck a good thing?"

Blake grunted as he held tight to the reins. Wreck a good thing? How was he supposed to wreck something good before it even began?

CHAPTER SEVENTEEN

Ashley spent the next few days by her grandfather's side, learning the ropes before he headed south for a fishing trip with some of his old friends. She used the time wisely, making notes about what to look for during the next few weeks and making sure she understood what to do if something went wrong.

"I think you should be good while I'm gone," her grandfather said. He had spent most of the morning packing and making phone calls to his clients. Ashley couldn't help but wonder how Blake felt about her grandfather leaving for vacation. "The winter months can get pretty rough here on the ranch, but as long as you keep a close eye on things, it'll be alright."

Ashley nodded as she looked down at her notes. There was nothing on the list she couldn't handle.

"I'll only be a phone call away, Ash," her grandfather said, pulling her attention away from the paper in her hands. Her eyes met his, and he offered a reassuring smile as he reached out to hug her. Thoughts of his last episode crossed her mind, and she could only pray he would stay safe during his vacation. "Besides, you'll have Blake and the other boys to help if things don't go as planned. Blake knows quite a bit around here. He's been watching me ever since he was Brycen's age."

Ashley thought about the history of the ranch and how long her grandfather had been working there. The Dixon family seemed to adore her grandfather. They'd accepted him as one of their own family members over the years.

"How are things going with you and Blake anyhow?"

Her grandfather's eyes focused on her as he waited for an honest answer. Ashley offered a subtle shrug. Knowing it wouldn't be enough to satisfy his curiosity, she said, "He seems more relaxed now with the idea of having us here at the ranch. Brycen really likes him, too."

Her grandfather's eyes lit up as his lips pulled into a smile. "I knew the two of them would be good for one another," he said. He nudged her in the arm with his elbow and said, "I've heard through the grapevine that you really like him too, huh?"

Ashley's cheeks flushed. She hadn't talked to her grandfather about their budding relationship. She'd talked about Blake and Brycen's trip to the creek and how much Brycen looked up to Blake. Which her grandfather had already known would happen in a matter of time. Her grandfather seemed to know quite a bit, and Ashley always appreciated his input.

"No need for words, Ash," her grandfather said, pulling Ashley from her distracted thoughts. "Your face says it all."

Her grandfather laughed as he gently nudged her. "Blake's a good man. He may seem a little rough around the edges, but he's got a big heart and takes care of those he loves the most."

Ashley nodded as her thoughts went back to the other night. He'd seemed so distant, guarded even, at the table. He'd heard Brycen loud and clear, and that's what caused him to leave that night. She'd wanted to talk with him after supper, but he'd left before she said anything at all.

"Well, I'm going to check on Sweet Pea and the other calves around here," her grandfather said, offering her a quick hug before stepping around her. "If you see Blake before I do, let him know I'll be heading out sometime after lunch."

Ashley nodded. "Will do."

Her grandfather walked past Blake's desk with scattered papers strewn about and stopped at the door.

"Don't worry about a thing, Ash. Everything's going to be alright."

Ashley smiled, trusting her grandfather was right. Things hadn't been easy for her and Brycen, but as long as they had people who cared about them and loved them, Ashley knew they would be just fine.

"Love you, kiddo," her grandfather said with a wink as he opened the office door and stepped outside.

Ashley smiled and said, "Love you, too, Gramps."

She watched as her grandfather headed for the barn. A part of her wanted to follow him, but there was a part of her that wanted to wait for Blake to walk into the office and find her there. Ashley wanted to see his reaction when he saw her sitting in his office. She wanted to talk about what he'd heard Brycen say.

She looked at the clock on the wall and realized it was just after ten. Blake usually completed his morning routine around nine thirty and should make his way to the office any minute now.

Ashley sat down at the desk Blake had given her. She busied herself with the mindless task of organizing unpaid invoices and scattered receipts. After Blake had asked her to work part-time on the books, Ashley spent a few hours a day in his office. She still hadn't found the discrepancy they'd been looking for, but she was getting closer.

The sound of footsteps echoed against the wooden planks out front of the administration building, causing Ashley to look up from the papers she'd been passing the time studying. Blake opened the office door and stepped inside, his eyes meeting hers before looking away. "I didn't think you'd be here," Blake said. There was something in the way he'd said the words that caused Ashley's heart to sink. Was he trying to avoid her?

She straightened in the chair and shuffled the papers into a neat pile before turning around, giving him her full attention. "I'm sorry. I met Gramps here after sending Brycen off to school. We were going over things I needed to be prepared for while he's gone."

Her heart raced as she watched Blake. He slid into the chair at his desk, making no attempt to look at her. She wanted to bolt. She wanted to run out of the office and never look back.

Blake thumbed through a few papers in front of him. "Yeah, he said he's heading south for a few weeks."

Ashley swallowed past the lump in her throat. It was more than obvious Blake didn't want her there. The small office was crowded as it was, even without adding suffocating tension to it. "I should get going. I have a few things I want to check on before he leaves this afternoon."

She stood from her chair, prepared to make a run for it.

"Ash, wait," Blake said, reaching out to her as she made her way to the door. Her breath caught in her throat as his hand touched her skin. "We need to talk."

She released a slow breath in a failed attempt to calm her nerves. Her heart raced, knowing what was coming. She couldn't blame him. Things had happened so fast, neither of them were prepared to cross the line.

He released his hold on her arm and looked away before saying, "I don't think this is going to work out."

Ashley took a step back, waiting for the other shoe to drop. Everything would change in an instant if he no longer wanted her there on the ranch. Not to mention the breaking of her heart... and Brycen's heart as well.

"I think we got a little too ahead of ourselves, to be honest," Blake said as he tapped a pen against a stack of papers. "I know you need to be here to finish your schooling—"

"But?" Ashley choked out, trying her best to keep it together while her world seemed to crash around her. "Blake, I know you heard what Brycen said the other night. I can only imagine how it made you feel."

Blake leaned back in his chair, a hard look pressed on his face as he crossed his arms over his chest. He was guarding himself. Putting up a wall between them. Stepping back from what could have been a wonderful thing. Ashley's heart plummeted and her stomach dropped.

"I can't have him thinking that I'm trying to replace his father, Ash," Blake said. He turned to look at her now, his dark eyes piercing through her. "That's the last thing I want to do."

Ashley took a step back. She came to the Dixon Ranch looking for a job but received so much more than that. She found a place to live and raise Brycen. She was among several people she now called friends. They had welcomed her with open arms, making her feel right at home.

"Brycen knows you're not," Ashley argued, fearing that Blake had already made up his mind. "I talked with him and told him everything would be okay. Isn't that what you said?"

A flash of recognition sparked concern in Blake's eyes before he looked away from her. He mindlessly thumbed through a stack of papers that sat on the edge of his desk. Ashley stepped toward him, closing the distance between them. "Is ending this what you really want, Blake?"

"I don't know what I want," Blake said. "I just know that it's complicated and I don't need a ten-year-old getting hurt when things go wrong."

Ashley paused and reflected on his statement before saying, "Who says things will go wrong?"

Blake removed his hat and tossed it beside him on the desk. He ran a hand through his hair and shook his head. "No one said anything. I just know how things will go once you decide you don't like it here anymore."

Ashley was taken aback by his assumption. "What gave you the impression that I don't like it here? I've been through thick and thin around here, trying my best to fit in and get the job done. The last thing on my mind is leaving."

Blake remained silent, making it easy for her to continue on with how she truly felt—even if he wouldn't believe her. "Brycen and I needed a fresh start. Somewhere I could raise him while finishing out my dreams and coping with our loss without the daily reminder. My grandpa insisted we move here, and not once did I hesitate even while knowing there was a chance it might not work out."

Blake took a step back and sat on the edge of his desk. Before he questioned her, she said, "I know you think that I'm just some city girl who will change her mind when things get tough, but I'm not."

"I don't think—"

"I'm not like the others, Blake," she stated matter-of-factly. "Trust me. The last thing I expected to do when we moved here was to find a place to call home and fall in love. Falling was the last thing I wanted to do, but you gave me no choice. The only thing I prayed for was a smooth transition, at least for Brycen's sake."

He might have said something given the chance, but she didn't let him have it. She turned and walked out of the office before he called after her. If he wanted to end things, she wouldn't stand there arguing with him. He'd already made up his mind. She didn't have to like his decision, and she couldn't make him change his mind about her.

Ashley retraced her footsteps back to the calving barn as she walked through the fallen snow. The winds had picked up, blowing in the first real snowstorm of the year. Her grandfather would make his way out of town just in time to miss it.

She pushed past the barn door, entering the building in search of her grandfather. Maybe Blake was right... maybe they had taken things too fast. Maybe it was better to call it quits before something went wrong.

She rounded the paneling separating the orphaned calf from the others. She needed to clear her thoughts and calm down before she did something foolish—like call it quits and leave the ranch.

Ashley stepped into the warm pen after grabbing a

bottle of milk and found a clean spot next to the calf. The two of them had formed a special bond over the last few days, and Ashley was more than proud of taking care of Sweet Pea.

"Are you hungry, little one?" she questioned as she held up the bottle in front of the calf. She and Brycen had made it a point to check on Sweet Pea and the others quite often as the early-winter weather rolled into Montana. Ashley found it hard to believe that just a few short weeks ago, they'd arrived on the ranch and had fit right in. A lot had happened since their first day, and Ashley couldn't help but think about what Blake had said. Did he really believe that she would quit on her grandfather, not to mention Blake, and leave the ranch?

Ashley rested her head back against the paneling of the pen and closed her eyes as she fed the calf. Everything had seemed to go so well. What had caused Blake to change his mind? Brycen couldn't have been the only reason Blake wanted to put a stop to their relationship. Something told her that Blake must have experienced a hurtful breakup in the past to make him doubt her love for him.

"Hey," her grandfather called out as he peeked over the edge of the wooden panel. "I didn't think I'd find you out here."

Ashley looked up, meeting her grandfather's

concern with a half-hearted smile. "I just wanted to take a break from the office for a minute or two."

Her grandfather unlatched the door and let himself in. He grabbed an empty bucket and flipped it over before sitting down next to Ashley. "I don't know how you can spend so much time looking at the computer screen, anyway."

She didn't want to admit that having Blake in the office made it easier, at least until recently anyway. She offered a subtle shrug and exchanged the bottle with her other hand. The calf had drunk half the milk in the time she'd spent lost in her thoughts.

"I've always liked working with numbers and banking," she admitted confidently. She'd spent her time working as a bookkeeper for a small business in the heart of the city she lived in. It had given her something to fill her time while trying to figure out how to finish her schooling. "It helps pass the time around here."

Her grandfather studied her for a minute before asking, "Why do I get the feeling that you're not happy?"

She tried her best to convince her grandfather otherwise. The last thing she wanted was for him to think that she wasn't sticking around. It was bad enough to have Blake think that, let alone her grandfather.

"Did something happen that I should know about?" her grandfather questioned, refusing to let it go. "Is Blake having second thoughts again? You just need to tell him to settle down and not worry about the future for once."

Ashley couldn't bring herself to tell her grandfather it had nothing to do with the ranch and everything to do with the relationship she and Blake had rushed into.

"No, nothing happened at all," Ashley said, offering her grandfather a reassuring smile. No sooner had the calf finished the bottle than Ashley caught her grandfather checking the time on his watch. "Are you late for your date with the guys?"

Her grandfather cracked a smile, and she found herself relieved to have changed the subject. She didn't need her grandfather worrying about her or Brycen while he was enjoying himself on vacation. He'd earned the trip, and he needed a break from the business side of things.

"What do you say we head inside and grab some lunch?" he asked, standing in the spot next to her. He held out a hand and helped her to her feet. Ashley brushed off the loose cedar chips and clumps of bedding that clung to the back of her jeans. "I'd like to get my belly full before I venture out too far on my own."

Ashley agreed to join him for lunch, fully aware that she would see Blake at the dinner table. She could only hope that things wouldn't get too awkward between them now that he'd called it quits on their burgeoning relationship.

CHAPTER EIGHTEEN

Blake finished scanning the last few receipts left in the file from the middle of spring. He had yet to find the discrepancy, and it was driving him crazy. Not to mention the fact that he was trying to concentrate after ending things with Ashley.

He'd seen the look on her face as she'd let him have it. He felt bad for ending their relationship, but he had to do what he felt was best. He'd been there before, and it hadn't ended well. Of course, his last relationship hadn't involved a kid. The last thing he wanted was to break a child's heart.

Blake tapped the pen against the next stack of papers he needed to look over. He figured it was best to lie low for a while. He planned to stay in the office most of the day and skip out on lunch with the family.

To be honest, he wanted to avoid seeing Ashley.

She was upset with him, and she had every right to be. He'd give it a few days and wait for things to cool down before approaching her again.

He thought about having her in his office. How difficult it would be if she worked alongside him after ending their relationship. Thoughts of her crossed his mind several times throughout the afternoon, distracting him from getting anything figured out.

Maybe he would get lucky and Ashley would keep her distance as well.

The slamming of the door, followed by heavy footsteps, pulled Blake's attention from the stack of invoices in front of him. He turned, realizing it was his mother who was now standing behind him with a concerned look on her face while holding a plate of food.

"It's not like you to skip out on lunch," she said, offering him the plate. "I figured I'd find you elbow-deep in work."

He offered a half-smile as he accepted the food. "Thanks, Ma."

When he realized she was waiting for an explanation why he hadn't come inside, he informed her that the books were driving him crazy. Of course, she wouldn't accept his reasoning. And it didn't take long for her to find the empty chair at Ashley's desk before sitting down.

"I thought you gave the bookkeeping to Ashley,"

she stated, leaving no room to argue with her. Blake nodded, knowing his mother knew better than to think otherwise. "I did, but you know how I am when it comes to getting things figured out. I wanted to take another look for myself and see if I'd missed something."

His mother studied him from across the room. "Well, why don't you call on Curt and see if maybe he can help you figure it out?"

"I'm not sure Curt's the one to blame for this mixup," Blake stated, focusing back on the stack in front of him. "I mean, it's possible that he might have paid for something without noting it in the books, which caused me to pay for it twice…"

Blake flipped through the papers inside another file. He'd looked through these files repeatedly while coming up short on an answer. "It's crazy to think that I caused the ranch to go into the red."

His mother leaned back and crossed her arms in front of her. Blake hadn't told her about the foreclosure notice from the bank. He'd taken a second mortgage on the ranch to purchase their third round of heifers from another rancher soon after Curt left. He wouldn't have done so if he had realized they couldn't afford it.

"What do you mean in the red?" A look of concern crossed his mother's face as she tried to figure out what Blake wasn't telling her. He wanted to tell her everything would be okay. That there wasn't anything to worry about. That it was just a fluke in record keeping, and he would get it all sorted out. "Blake, what's going on?"

"Aside from thinking I had everything figured out and failing?"

Blake choked on his honesty, knowing his mother would see right through him. He was ashamed at believing he could handle the ranch after Curt left. The thought of disappointing his family while failing to make his father proud ricocheted through his mind. Failing to uphold his father's ranch was as painful as a knife in the chest—if not worse.

"You're not failing," his mother assured him as she stood from the chair and walked over to him. "It's just time you asked someone for help. I'm sure Curt wouldn't mind coming over and taking a look in order to figure things out. He managed things just fine before deciding to hand it off to you boys."

His mother was right. His uncle Curt had kept the ranch running with no trouble after the Dixon brothers lost their father. Curt had left his own life in Maple Glen and moved to Montana in order to help Blake's family through the tough times.

"And the last thing you need to worry about is making your father proud," his mother scolded. "Your father was more than proud of the three of you, and nothing will ever change that. He may not be here today to say it for himself, but I can attest to it. If he were standing right here in this office, in this very spot, he would tell you how proud you've made him."

Blake looked away from his mother, ashamed to have brought it up. Losing their father hadn't only affected the Dixon brothers, it had taken a toll on their mother as well. She'd done her best to hold the family together and had carried them through the tragic loss of their father.

His thoughts flashed to Ashley and how she'd done the same for Brycen. She was only trying to do what was best for her and Brycen. Falling in love with him hadn't been in her plans when they came to the ranch. He'd been selfish to make everything about him.

"Listen," his mother said, pulling him from deep thought. "You go ahead and eat lunch. I'll give Curt a call and ask him to stop by when he has a minute."

Blake sat in his chair and said nothing for a couple of minutes. His mother tugged on the sleeve of his flannel, tearing his attention away from his distracting thoughts. "Okay?"

"Alright," he said, agreeing to let Curt look at the books. Maybe his uncle would know right where to look—pinpointing a minute detail Blake might have overlooked. "Thanks, Ma."

She pulled him into a side hug and patted him on the back before planting a kiss on his cheek. "Sometimes it's okay to let go of the reins a little and allow people in to help. Not everyone has bad intentions, Blake." His mother stepped away from his desk and gave him a knowing look. One that told him she'd figured out the real reason he'd skipped out on lunch. "You've got to have a little faith that things will work out without having to worry and control every aspect of your life. Sometimes you just have to listen to your heart and let things just be."

She offered a soft smile as she reached the door. Before stepping out of the office, she turned back to face Blake one last time and said, "I hope you'll think twice about ending things out of fear with Ashley, Blake. She's the last one I'd suspect to break your heart. Not when hers is just as fragile."

A FEW HOURS LATER, BLAKE HEADED OUT TO THE barn, ready to clear his mind and free his thoughts. He had a lot of things circling around inside of his mind and the last thing he wanted to do was sit around and wait for Curt to show up.

He walked to the stables and secured Chance's saddle before climbing onto the back of the horse. No matter how trying things could be, Blake always found peace by taking a break with a quick horseback ride.

He'd scanned the property for Ashley, feeling disappointed when he didn't catch sight of her. Even though he'd told himself to lie low for a while, he couldn't help but think about her and Brycen. There was no doubt he'd been a fool to blame overhearing Brycen's thoughts as his reason for wanting to end things with Ashley. Having a family of his own one day had been something he'd hoped for quite often. More so now that his brothers had each found love and settled down.

Blake guided Chance away from the barn, looking for Ashley one last time before trotting off toward the mountains. It would do him good to get some fresh air. The snowstorm that had threatened to hang around for a while had been long gone soon after Blake had eaten his lunch. There was no time like the present to become one with nature and pray to God for guidance and understanding.

"Mind if we join you?" Garrett called out from a nearby building. His brothers rode up alongside Blake on their horses and offered him a sly grin. If he didn't know any better, he'd think they were up to no good.

"Looks like I might not have a choice," Blake answered amusingly.

They trotted alongside Blake in silence, making him wonder what the two of them were up to. Not that it wasn't common for the three of them to ride out into the mountains together. It was just the fact

Garrett was looking mischievous with a Cheshire cat grin lining his face.

"Okay, spill it," Blake stated, pulling on the reins and coming to a halt at the edge of their property.

"Spill what?" Drew asked, grinning as he looked from Garrett to Blake. "I have nothing to spill other than the fact we heard what happened this morning."

Blake let out a low grunt and shifted his weight in the saddle. The last thing he needed was for his brothers to hear about ending things with Ashley. They'd given him grief time and time again for not taking a chance on love after his last failed relationship—even though that hadn't been his fault. She'd led him on to believe she was happy on the ranch... until she wasn't and it became glaringly obvious. The day Melanie left the ranch, he gave up his hopes and dreams of marrying the love of his life and raising a family on the ranch.

"Who told you?" Blake growled as he looked from one brother to the next.

Garrett let out a slight laugh and shook his head. "No one had to tell us anything. It was written all over Ashley's face when she came in for lunch."

"Not to mention, the two of you haven't spent an hour apart since she first got here," Drew added, "at least not until today."

Blake focused on the snow-covered trees surrounding them as he tried to think of something to say. He played it off like they were looking too far into it. "So because I skipped lunch today, that means what, exactly?" he asked with a light chuckle. "Get out of here."

Garrett led his horse in front of Blake and called out, "We know you better than to believe you'd miss out on lunch without good reason."

Blake shot a look from Garrett to Drew, who offered a slight shrug as if to say he agreed with their brother. "You two are something else, you know that?"

He nudged Chance in the side, encouraging the horse to move forward. Drew and Garrett exchanged glances, but said nothing more about what they thought happened between Blake and Ashley.

Garrett slowed his horse as he pointed out a gathering of deer running along the edge of the river. "Looks like they're moving down from the mountains," he called out over his shoulder. "I'd hate to think about what they're running from."

Blake and Drew came to a stop next to Garrett and studied the deer in the clearing of the woods. There was no doubt the same pack of wolves that had wreaked havoc on the ranch not too long ago was causing an uproar with the deer as they prowled the woods for their next meal.

"As long as they don't lead them back to our ranch, I'm okay with that."

His brothers offered nods in agreement with Blake's statement. Blake didn't wish a bad outcome on any animal, but if nature running its course meant saving their cattle from being attacked back at the ranch, he wouldn't be the one to complain.

The ride to the edge of the mountains went peacefully without having to talk any more about it. Blake had done what he'd done, and there was no going back now. He might feel bad about calling things off with Ashley, but at least for now, he wouldn't have to worry about losing more than just the ranch.

CHAPTER NINETEEN

As soon as Brycen got off the bus, he was busy talking Ashley's ear off about helping on the ranch when he got older. He mentioned talking to Blake and how Blake liked the idea of having another boy on the ranch. The hope of Brycen working on the ranch made Blake happy. Ashley didn't have the heart to tell him that the future of living on the ranch was up in the air.

She would have liked to believe nothing would ever stop them from living there. It had all seemed too good to be true when they'd first arrived at the Dixon Ranch. Working alongside her grandfather was a blessing in disguise, but deep down she knew that even that would be short-lived. She expected her grandfather to announce his retirement no sooner than he arrived home from vacation.

She wasn't ready to work with the animals alone. From the beginning, Blake had questioned her ability to competently complete ongoing tasks with the livestock. It didn't matter how many books she'd read over the last couple of weeks, she couldn't shake the overwhelming doubt bottling up inside of her.

"Do you care if I go play with Allie, Mom?"

Brycen's question pulled her out of the fog as he tugged on the sleeve of her winter coat. She couldn't tell him no. Not after the long day she'd had at the ranch. She would take a couple of hours to herself and curl up in front of the fireplace with a warm blanket and a delightful book—something not related to cattle and veterinary medicine.

"Sure, go ahead, but I want you to be careful and stay nearby," Ashley said, giving her son a quick hug before watching him run off toward Drew and Becca's cabin. They all lived close to one another, given just a short distance in between each cabin and cottage. Everyone worked together to keep a close eye on the kids. It truly took a village to raise a kid these days. Ashley would be forever grateful for making memories with everyone at the ranch—even if the moments had been short-lived.

She followed the snow-covered gravel to her cabin, looking over her shoulder and relishing in the laughter of the children playing behind her. Brycen was teaching Allie how to make a snowman, but the snow was still too soft to stick together.

Ashley climbed the porch steps and looked around. She hadn't seen Blake a single time since meeting him in the office earlier that morning. Although she had kept herself busy for most of the morning and into the afternoon, she'd sent her grandfather off on his adventure with a sandwich bag full of fresh-baked cookies and extra love right after finishing lunch.

"Hey, Mom, look," Brycen called out to her as he tossed a snowball at Allie. Ashley laughed when Allie didn't take more than a minute to gather snow in her little gloved hands before giving it right back to him. "Ah, man," Brycen groaned, shaking the snow from the hood of his coat. "That's cold."

Allie's laughter echoed around them, flowing freely in the crisp winter air. "Told you I can make snowballs," she called out, threatening to get Brycen with another one before he ran away from her.

Ashley smiled and offered a quick wave before heading inside. The kids would be fine playing in the snow for a little while longer. When they were cold and ready to come inside, Ashley would have mugs of hot chocolate for them.

No sooner had Ashley draped the afghan over her lap and curled up with a book than a knock sounded at the front door. At first, she thought it might have been the kids horsing around and playing jokes on her. But after the second knock came a sweet and familiar voice from the other side of the door.

"Ash, are you home?"

Ashley marked her place in the book and tossed the blanket to the side before hurrying to the door. Mama Dixon greeted Ashley with a warm smile as she held a freshly baked pie in her mittened hands. "I figured I'd brighten your day with a homemade pie," Mama Dixon said as she held the pie up in front of her and offered it to Ashley. "The day has been so gloomy with all of this snow, I couldn't help but bake up some fresh pies."

Ashley kindly accepted the offering as she invited Mama Dixon inside. Mama Dixon stepped inside and slipped off her oversized winter coat before hanging it on a nearby hook. "I also brought a bottle of wine if you'd like to have a glass with me?"

Ashley walked into the kitchen and placed the pie on the counter before turning and reaching into a nearby cabinet for her wine glasses. The last time she had wine was long before Colin got sick. They had celebrated their wedding anniversary by deciding to stay home and enjoy the evening together—just the two of them, with a bottle of wine and a good movie.

She quickly dismissed the memory with a heartfelt smile as she retraced her steps back to the counter and set the glasses down in front of Mama Dixon, who was prepared to pour the wine.

"It's so good to see little Brycen and Allie getting along so well," Mama Dixon said, lifting the glass to her lips and taking a sip. Ashley agreed as she led Mama Dixon into the living room and offered her a place to sit down next to her on the couch. "I love the idea of having grandchildren here on the ranch. Seeing my boys become fathers will always make my heart happy."

Ashley admired the amount of love Mama Dixon had for her family. The woman reminded her of her own mother when she carried on about her children and future grandchildren.

"You know," Mama Dixon said, setting her glass down on a coaster next to her and getting situated just right on the cushion next to Ashley. "I'd always thought Blake would be the first to settle down and raise himself a family of his own."

Ashley offered a half-smile, uncertain with where Mama Dixon was taking the conversation. She didn't want to talk about Blake and the future his mother thought he would have. Not when everything went up in smoke less than twelve hours ago. "I think all mothers expect that with their children."

Mama Dixon acknowledged Ashley's statement with a smile before saying, "I know things haven't always been easy... for either of you, and I know Blake has a lot of fear when it comes to falling in love."

"Oh, well, that's okay," Ashley said as she lifted the glass of wine to her lips. The last thing she wanted was to talk about Blake with his own mother. What happened this morning was over and done with. Ashley should have known better than to allow herself the chance to fall in love with someone like Blake to begin with—stubborn and rough around the edges. "Would you like a piece of pie?"

Ashley set her glass down on the end table and stood up from the couch. It was a failed attempt at changing the subject because Mama Dixon followed her right over to the counter and continued on with the conversation.

"I guess what I'm trying to say is," Mama Dixon said, reaching out a hand to stop Ashley from cutting into the pie. Ashley set the knife on the counter, easing the distraction from conversation, and looked up at Mama Dixon. It didn't matter whether Ashley wanted to hear it. Though she figured whatever Mama Dixon said might be worth hearing if it would give Ashley any advice or direction with Blake. "Blake likes to know what's going to happen before it happens. He's the one who takes hold of the reins when everyone else lets go of them. But that doesn't mean he doesn't worry or have any fears."

Ashley knew that much about Blake already. She'd known that from the day she'd first met him. He liked to have full control of what he could, and he was a bit too stubborn to let go and let someone else in.

"He cares about you and Brycen, Ash," Mama Dixon stated matter-of-factly. "I've seen it in the way he looks at you and watches after Brycen. He might have ended things with you this morning, but I know deep down that's the last thing he wanted to do."

Ashley looked away from Mama Dixon, not sure why the woman insisted Blake loved her when he'd given up so easily. It made little sense to Ashley. If he cared that much, he would have given them time. He would have talked with her about what he feared the most instead of ending it.

"I know I can't speak for Blake," Mama Dixon said, breaking the silence between them. "He's a grown man who can speak for himself. I just wanted you to know that we all love having you here at the ranch and would hate to see you leave just because Blake reacted to his fear of getting hurt again. You're welcome to stay here at the ranch for however long you'd like. No matter what happens from this day forward."

Ashley nodded, accepting Mama Dixon's offer. She wouldn't admit to thinking about leaving the ranch once she completed her internship with her grandfather. That point in her life was months—years, really—down the road. Who knew what the future would bring for her and Brycen? She could only hope whatever it brought, they would manage well enough alone.

CHAPTER TWENTY

"Bev says you're wanting me to take a look at the books?"

Blake turned around at the sound of his uncle's voice behind him. "Yeah, something isn't adding up, and I'm having a hard time figuring it out," Blake admitted. "I received a notice from the bank, but I thought we were already paid up until next year. Not to mention, I made the payment to the county for property taxes, which took the ranch into the red."

Curt stepped into the office and closed the door behind him. He approached Blake's desk and looked over Blake's shoulder at the notes lying sporadically in front of him. It made little sense that the bank had sent the letter, warning them of a past due balance when Blake could have sworn they were current on payments.

"Did you call the bank and ask if they received the payment?" Curt asked, pulling up a chair next to Blake's desk. "I know I sent them a check for the year's worth of payments soon after writing a check for the taxes and insurance."

Blake shook his head. "Are you sure you sent them a check? Maybe you thought you did and only wrote it down in the books like you had," Blake said, scanning the sheets in front of him and checking once again for the discrepancy. They could run in the red for a while as long as payments were both made to the bank and to the county. Blake had plans to make up the year's losses with the profit he'd brought in from the cattle this year. What he couldn't afford was the foreclosing of the ranch to the bank for the missed payments.

"Let me take a look and see what might've gone wrong," Curt said as he motioned for Blake to pass him the papers so he could look at the spreadsheet. Blake watched Curt as he studied the past year and a half's worth of records and waited for his uncle to come up with something Blake had overlooked. Something that would end his frustrations and worry about losing the ranch.

After spending thirty minutes looking over everything, Curt tapped a finger against the paper he gripped in his hand. "Right here," he said, leaning forward and holding the sheet out for Blake to get a better look. Check numbers, followed by the payment amounts, filled the column of a printed spreadsheet as Curt held up another beside it. "It looks like I might not have sent them the check like I'd thought."

Blake leaned back in his chair and ran a hand through his hair. If his uncle hadn't written the check to the bank, that would explain the letter he had received, but that didn't explain why they were running in the red. What happened to the money that was supposed to go to the bank?

"Are you sure you didn't write any checks without writing them down in the books first?" There had to be something that was paid without accounting for it, or something had to have been paid twice. The only thing Blake could think of, after exhausting all the other thoughts, was having paid more than once or twice to cover the property taxes and insurance. That would equal out the amount of the mortgage, but put them in the red with the extra to taxes and insurance. "Let me look at something real quick."

He grabbed the papers back from Curt and looked them over. It didn't seem possible that he would have overlooked such an obvious discrepancy, but then again, with everything happening at the ranch with the wolves and the herd, not to mention Ashley and

Brycen, Blake had been well beyond distracted over the last few weeks.

"What do you think might have happened?" Curt asked, leaning forward and resting his arms on the desk in front of him.

Blake flipped through the sheets, comparing the amounts from one column to the next. He took an extra look at the timing because it was all making sense to him as he put the pieces together. "Well, I think I just solved the mystery," Blake said, tapping his pen against the paper in his hand. "It looks like before you left, you must have written down that you had paid the bank, but you must not have sent the check, or if you did, they didn't receive it somehow."

Blake chose his words carefully. The last thing he wanted was for his uncle to think Blake was accusing him of intentionally skewing the books. "But then we hired that accountant, who I thought knew what she was doing," Blake explained, inspecting the dates printed on the spreadsheet. "But, from the looks of it, we paid an extra three payments to property taxes and insurance while allowing the bank payment to fall through the cracks."

Curt ran a hand through his salt-and-pepper gray hair and offered an apologetic nod. "I'm sorry that got overlooked. A simple mistake that can be corrected with an online payment to the bank today."

Blake thought about how things had seemed to

run smoothly when he didn't know the mess it caused by having three different people look after the books. Going forward, he would make sure it wouldn't happen again. He was confident he and Ashley could rectify the situation going forward, but first, he needed to figure out how he'd pay the bank.

"That's easier said than done when we're looking at a negative balance even after adding back the unpaid amount to the bank in the first place," Blake stated, worrying how they would make things right with the bank while running in the red. The bank wouldn't wait until spring to foreclose the ranch. They wouldn't care to hear the reasoning behind the missed payments, or how much of a profit Blake expected come spring after selling their Angus cattle.

Curt sat back in his chair as Blake continued to correct the mistakes in the books. It had been a glaringly obvious discrepancy that he'd missed time and time again. No matter how distracted he'd become in the last few months, he should have caught the mistake before writing any more checks.

"I've got enough to cover the payment," Curt said with confidence. Blake looked at his uncle like he'd lost his mind. There was no way Blake would allow Curt to pay for the mishap. When Blake shook his head, Curt insisted he let him make things right. "It was my mistake to begin with. And you were only doing what you knew was right after taking over the place."

No matter what his uncle said, or how much blame he was willing to take, Blake couldn't let his uncle fork over that kind of money. "I'll figure out a way to make it work. I'll call the bank and see if they'll work with me—"

"You don't need to do all that," Curt said, leaning forward and looking Blake in the eye. "I'm telling you, I've got it covered. It's no sweat off my back. I want to make sure you and the rest of the bunch are taken care of."

Blake couldn't argue with his uncle. He felt the weight of things lift off his chest the minute Curt made the offer. "I'll pay you back come spring. I'll be sure to pay you as soon as the first check rolls in."

Curt shook his head and dismissed Blake's offer with a wave of his hand. "There's no need to do all that," he said. "I'm not too worried about it. It's the least I can do."

Blake ran a relaxed hand through his hair and leaned back in his chair. It all seemed too easy after all the months of worrying and stress it had caused. If his uncle was more than willing to help him out, the least he could do was thank him and make sure it didn't happen again.

Blake spent the next few days making things right with the books. He spent most of his spare time in his office, looking over at the empty desk across from him and thinking about Ashley. There was no doubt he had hurt her when he'd ended things with her. He hadn't talked to her since that morning. Lying low had been his plan, and it had worked. His brothers were giving him a hard time, and his mother mentioned taking a pie to Ashley the other day. But he couldn't bring himself to talk about the reason he'd done what he did.

Spending time away from Ashley hadn't made him feel any better, unlike how he thought he'd feel after letting go of what they had. Blake thought about Ashley more often than not—no matter how busy he kept himself around the ranch. Everything reminded him of her and Brycen.

All his life, he'd hoped and prayed for a family of his own one day. He wanted to live the life his parents had made for themselves when they lived on the ranch together. Blake might have been too young to understand what love was before he lost his father, but he'd been old enough to see the love his parents shared with one another.

He couldn't have what he wanted unless he let go of his need to control everything—including his own future. His need to control everything was the one thing that created his fear of losing everything he cared about and loved the most. He didn't need anyone to tell him that. He lived with it every day.

His fear of losing the ranch and failing at making his father proud while following in his footsteps weren't the only two things holding him back. He was afraid of losing the ones he loved the most. Not only his family, but Ashley and Brycen, too. They could be here one day and gone the next. Life was unpredictable, and he couldn't take the chance of going through that kind of heartbreak again.

Or at least, that's what he once believed. He had no reason to let go of Ashley and Brycen just because he feared losing them. Life was too short to sit back and wait for something bad to happen.

Blake tapped his pen against the desk as he stared at the empty chair across from him. He hadn't accepted Ashley's presence on the ranch at first, but all of that changed when he had taken the time to know her—and Brycen.

The young boy he'd bonded with was afraid of Blake replacing his father. That was the last thing Blake wanted to do. Sure, he wanted to be there for both of them. He wanted to give them the life he had once hoped for while growing up on the ranch.

He would never want to fill the void in Ashley's and Brycen's hearts by replacing the man they'd shared so much with. All Blake wanted to do was be there for them and give them a life they could enjoy while taking care of them and loving them without hesitation or fear holding him back.

Blake pushed back his chair and made his way to the door. He grabbed his flannel jacket and cowboy hat from the hook and headed out into the brisk November winds and falling snow.

He wasn't sure what he would say to Ashley when he got to her place, but none of that mattered. He would speak from his heart and tell her how much he wanted her and Brycen to be a part of his life. How much he wanted them to be a part of his ranch, and an even bigger part of his family.

There was no telling how the conversation would go or how Ashley would react. She could tell him she was planning to leave once finishing her internship, or she could tell him she was leaving today.

Blake could only hope that she would forgive him and tell him she would stay on the ranch for as long as he would let her. He'd let her stay there forever if that meant he wouldn't spend another day without her and Brycen in his life.

He trekked up the snow-covered gravel toward her cabin, praying that she would forgive him and understand that he'd said and done what he had out of fear.

Allie and Brycen played outside, chasing each other around in the front yard, as Blake approached Ashley's cabin. The kids stopped long enough to greet him before carrying on with their snow-filled activities.

He walked up the front porch steps, careful not to lose his footing as he approached the front door. The last thing he needed was to land head first into a snowbank when he made things right with Ashley.

Before he knocked, the wooden door swung open and Ashley appeared, carrying two coffee mugs filled to the brim with hot chocolate and marshmallows.

"Blake," she breathed as she took a step back. "I—"

"I know I'm the last person you're expecting to see right now," Blake said, interrupting her before giving her a chance to send him away. "But I wanted to stop by and tell you how sorry I am that—"

"It's okay."

She said it with such a confidence that Blake almost believed her, but he knew better than that. It wasn't okay. And it wouldn't be until he made things right.

"Ash," he said as he stepped to the side so she could set the mugs down on the porch railing. The kids raced up the porch steps and grabbed their drinks, not giving them time to cool off. Blake smiled as he watched them enjoy something he had at their age. Nothing was better than a cup of hot chocolate and marshmallows after playing in the snow.

He turned his attention back to Ashley. Sure,

seeing the kids happy and making memories was something he enjoyed, but that wasn't why he was there.

Blake took a step toward Ashley, careful not to step on her slipper-clad feet, and reached out to her. He took a hold of her hand and heard her breath catch in her throat in response to his touch. "I'm sorry that I ended things how I did," he started, knowing it was now or never and there was no turning back. "I can tell you a million reasons, but all of those would sound like empty excuses."

Ashley relaxed as her gaze met his. Confusion and uncertainty filled her eyes, which made him regret making the mistake of letting her go. She would more than likely have a hard time believing that he cared about her and Brycen after what he'd done.

"I'm not here to justify my actions, because the Lord knows I've beat myself up enough over the last few days while thinking about you and Brycen," he said matter-of-factly. He drew her in close to him, closing the distance between them and said, "Ashley, I let fear take over after I heard what Brycen said to you that night. I thought it would have been easier if I stepped back and allowed the two of you space on the ranch without having me overstepping—"

"But you didn't overstep, Blake," Ashley said, still looking him in the eye. "You did nothing wrong.

And I know it must've been hard to hear how much we still love Colin and how much we miss him—"

"It was hard to hear, but that's not what bothered me, Ash," Blake said. "I didn't want to make Brycen feel like that. I mean, I want him to know that I'm here for you guys, and I always will be, but I never want him, or you, to feel like I'm trying to replace the man before me."

Ashley's eyes filled with tears as she melted into Blake's arms. He reached up and wiped away the fallen tears with his thumb as he looked her in the eye. "I want to love you, and have you love me, too, and Brycen…"

Blake looked over his shoulder at Brycen, who was busy drinking his hot chocolate and paying no mind to their conversation. "I want to be there for him when he needs someone to lean on. Someone to teach him how to throw a football and how to ask a girl on his first date."

Ashley raised a brow at that and shook her head. "I don't know about that last one, but I like how the rest sounds."

"Okay, so the dating will be a while down the road," Blake agreed. He wrapped his arms around her and pulled her closer to him, leaving no room between them now as he looked down at her. "I don't know what the future holds, and I'm still learning to loosen the reins a bit when it comes to having full control, but I know how much I love and care about you and Brycen, and I want nothing to change that. Ever."

"Ever?" Ashley questioned, tilting her head to the side as she studied him. "Like as in... forever?"

"Forever and ever," Blake said with a wholehearted smile. "That is, as long as you're okay with that?"

Ashley's eyes glistened with tears as she looked up at him. "I'm more than okay with that."

"You are?" Blake questioned, not sure why he felt compelled to doubt the love she had for him.

"I am," she said as she looked over at Brycen and Allie, who were standing in the snowbank watching them in silence. "And I'm sure Brycen is, too."

Blake turned around, releasing Ashley for just a minute to glance at Brycen. Brycen's face lit up with the biggest smile Blake had ever seen on the kid since the first day he'd met him.

"Are you two going to kiss or what?" Allie called out from beside Brycen.

Brycen shook his head and offered a subtle shrug as he mumbled, "Girls."

Blake and Ashley shared a laugh before their lips met and everything Blake had once hoped for seemed to come true.

EPILOGUE

"Are you sure you're not retiring?"

The question echoed around the table at suppertime the night Ashley's grandfather returned home from his fishing trip. He'd only been gone for a week instead of three, and much to Ashley's surprise, he hadn't retired like she'd thought he would.

"You can't get rid of me that easily," her grandfather said with a loud grunt following his words. "Why do you think I cut my trip short and came back?"

"To tell us you're retiring?" Allie announced as a puzzled look crossed her face. She turned to Becca and asked, "What does retiring mean, Mama?"

They all shared a laugh around the table, talking about Doc's fishing trip and recalling memories he'd made while working at the Dixon Ranch. Ashley felt relieved to know her grandfather wasn't going anywhere anytime soon. She had a lot of learning left to do, and a couple of years to finish her internship before she could practice on her own.

"Hey, Doc," Drew called out from the other end of the table. "Did you hear what happened while you were gone?"

Puzzled expressions exchanged around the table as everyone tried to figure out what Drew was referring to.

Ashley's grandfather leaned forward and rested his arms on the table before saying, "If I had to guess, it might have something to do with Big Red getting out of the pasture again? Or maybe it has to do with Brycen learning how to ride a horse?"

Her grandfather waggled his brows at Brycen, throwing her son into a fit of laughter. "No," Brycen said between giggles.

"Well, I don't think we have to worry about Big Red getting out for a long time now that we used some old material Curt had lying around in his backyard," Garrett said proudly. "At least, I hope not anyway."

Ashley's grandfather turned his attention to her and asked, "What'd I miss?"

Ashley offered a slight shrug, giving her grandfather a hard time.

"Oh, you know," Drew said, pointing a finger between Blake and Ashley. "These two finally decided to get along and agree on something for once."

Her grandfather kicked back in the chair and tossed his head back with a laugh. "I already knew that was going to happen. With time and a bit of hope, anything is possible nowadays."

Ashley exchanged a look with Blake. Admiration and love for her and his family filled his eyes. There were a lot of things she'd hoped for in her lifetime, but nothing came close to having a man love her and Brycen the way only Blake could after they lost Colin.

She would be forever grateful for her second chance at love and being able to find a place to call home for a second time around. She would thank God daily for giving her everything she'd ever hoped for and more, while knowing the best was yet to come.

"I love you," she mouthed to Blake as he looked her way.

He leaned in close, wrapping his arms around her, and whispered, "And I love you," before kissing her on the cheek and causing a commotion filled with excitement at the dinner table.

"Hey, don't forget about me," Brycen said, wiggling his way in between the two of them. Blake scooted back as Ashley made room for Brycen to join them.

Blake wrapped an arm around them both and said, "I could never forget about you, bud. I love you more than you could know and ever hope for."

ABOUT THE AUTHOR

Christina Butrum launched her writing career in 2015 with the release of The Fairshore Series.

Writing contemporary fiction, she brings realistic situations with swoon-worthy romance to the pages - allowing her readers to fall in love right along with the characters.

When she isn't busy writing, Christina enjoys spending time with her family. Christina Butrum looks forward to publishing many more books for her readers to enjoy.

www.authorchristinabutrum.com

Sign Up for Christina's Newsletter Here:

https://www.subscribepage.com/authorcbutrum
Join Christina's Group Here:
https://www.facebook.com/groups/
ButrumsBookBabes

- facebook.com/authorcbutrum
- twitter.com/authorcbutrum
- amazon.com/author/christinabutrum
- bookbub.com/profile/christina-butrum

ALSO BY CHRISTINA BUTRUM

FAIRSHORE SERIES
Second Chances

Unexpected Chances

Fair Chances

KATE'S DUET
Kate's Valentine

Kate's Forever

CEDAR VALLEY SERIES
All She Ever Wanted

Everything She Needed

All She Ever Desired

A MAPLE GLEN ROMANCE SERIES
It Takes Two

Coffee for Two

RSVP for Two

Room for Two

Lesson for Two

One plus Two

Christmas for Two

DIXON RANCH SERIES

The Cowboy's Home

The Cowboy's Heart

The Cowboy's Hope

THE COWBOYS OF PINE CREEK

A Pine Creek Homecoming - *Coming Soon!*

A Pine Creek Second Chance - *Coming Soon!*

A Pine Creek Summer - *Coming Soon!*

A Pine Creek Christmas Miracle - *Coming Soon!*

A Pine Creek Wedding - *Coming Soon!*

A Pine Creek Holiday - *Coming Soon!*

STANDALONE NOVELS

No Place Like Home - Love in Seattle

Saving Jenna

INTERCONNECTED NOVELLA

Sweet on Love - A Lover's Landing Novella

Starting Over in Silver Leaf Falls - A Silver Leaf Falls Novella

Falling for the Single Dad - Hopeless Romantics of Willow Ridge - Book 6

SWEET PROMISE PRESS NOVELS

Choosing Chelsea - A Gold Coast Retrievers Novel

No Time for Goodbyes - A No Brides Club Novel

No Time for Mistletoe - A No Brides Club Novel

Never miss a new release!

Sign up for Christina Butrum's newsletter:

https://www.subscribepage.com/authorcbutrum

Made in United States
North Haven, CT
21 December 2024